The Y(

The Young Engineers on the Gulf

by H. Irving Hancock

CHAPTER I

THE MYSTERY OF A BLACK NIGHT

"I wish I had brought my electric flash out here with me," muttered Harry Hazelton uneasily.

"I told you that you'd better do it," chuckled Tom Reade.

"But how could I know that the night would be pitch dark?" Harry demanded. "I don't know this gulf weather yet, and fifteen minutes ago the stars were out in full force. Now look at them!"

"How can I look at them?" demanded Tom, halting. "My flashlight won't pierce the clouds."

Reade halted on his dark, dangerous footway, and Harry, just behind him, uttered a sigh of relief and halted also.

"I never was in such a place as this before."

"You've been in many a worse place, though," rejoined Tom. "I never heard you make half as much fuss, either."

"I think something must be wrong with my head," ventured Harry.

"Undoubtedly," Tom Reade agreed cheerily.

"Hear that water," Harry went on, in a voice scarcely less disconsolate than before.

"Of course," nodded Tom. "But the water can hardly be termed a surprise. We both knew that the Gulf of Mexico is here. We saw it several times to-day."

The two young men stood on a narrow ledge of stone that jutted out of the water. This wall of stone was the first, outer or retaining wall of masonry—-the first work of constructing a great breakwater. At high tide, this ledge was just fourteen inches above the level surface of the Gulf of Mexico, and at the time of the above conversation it was within twenty minutes of high tide. The top of this wall of masonry was thirty inches wide, which made but a narrow footway for the two youths who, on a pitch black night, were more than half a mile out from shore.

On a pleasant night, for a young man with a steady head, the top of this breakwater wall did not offer a troublesome footpath. In broad daylight hundreds of laborers and masons swarmed over it, working side by side, or on scows and dredges alongside.

"Wait, and I'll show a light," volunteered Tom raising his foot-long flashlight.

Some seventy-five yards behind them a crawling snake-like figure flattened itself out on the top of the rock wall.

"Don't show the light just yet," pleaded Harry. "It might only make me more dizzy."

The flattened figure behind them wriggled noiselessly along.

"Just listen to the water," continued Hazelton. "Tom, I'm half-inclined to think that the water is roughening."

"I believe it is," agreed Tom.

"Fine time we'll have getting back, if a gale springs up from the southward," muttered Harry.

3

"See here, old fellow," interposed Tom vigorously, "you're not up to concert pitch to-night. Now, I'll tell you what I'll do——first of all, what *you'll* do. You sit right down flat on the top of the wall. Then I'll move on up forward and see what has been happening out there that should boom shoreward with such a racket. You stay right here, and I'll be back as soon as I've looked into the face of the mystery."

"What do you take me for?" Harry asked almost fiercely. "A baby? Or a cold-foot?"

"Nothing like it," answered Tom Reade with reassuring positiveness. "You're out of sorts, to-night. Your head, or your nerves, or some thing, has gone back on you, and you walk through this blackness with half a notion that you're going to walk over a precipice, or drop head-first into some danger. With such a feeling it would be cruelty to let you go forward, chum, and I'm not going to do it. I'll go alone."

The crouching figure to the rear of the young engineers quivered as though this separation of the two engineers on this black night was a thing devoutly to be desired.

"You're not going to do anything of the sort," retorted Harry Hazelton. "I'm going forward with you. I'm going to stick to you. All I wanted was a minute in which to brace myself. I've had that minute. Now get forward with you. I'm on your heels!"

Tom Reade shrugged his shoulders slightly. However, he did not object or argue, for he realized that his chum was sensitive over any circumstance that seemed to point to sudden failure of his courage.

"Come along, then," urged Tom. "Wait just a second, though. I'll flash the light ahead along the wall, to show you that it's all there, and just where it lies."

A narrow beam of light shot ahead as Tom pressed the spring of his pocket flash lamp.

A weird enough scene the night betrayed. In perspective the wall ahead narrowed, until the two sides seemed to come to a point. Back of all was the thick curtain of black that had settled down over the gulf. A little farther out, too, the water seemed rougher. There would seem to be hardly a doubt that a gale was brewing.

"Shut that light off!" Hazelton commanded, fighting to repress a shudder. "I can do better in the darkness. Now, go ahead, and I'll follow."

Tom started, but he went slowly now, feeling that this pace was more suited to the condition of his chum's nerves. Harry followed resolutely, though none but himself knew how much effort it took for him to keep on in the face of such a nameless yet terrible dread as now assailed him.

To the rear a bulky, hulking figure rose and stood erect. With the softest of steps this apparition of the night followed after them, until it stole along, ghost-like, just behind Hazelton. Then a huge arm was raised, threateningly, over Harry's head.

At that particular moment, as though insensibly warned, Hazelton stopped, half-wheeling. In the next second Harry bounded back just out of reach of the descending arm, the hand of which held something. But in that backward spring

4

Harry, in order to save himself from pitching into the water, was oblige to turn toward Reade.

"Tom!" exploded the young engineer. "Flash the light here quickly!"

In the instant, however, that Harry had sprung backward the figure had slipped noiselessly into the water to the left. As Reade wheeled about, throwing on the light, he let the ray fall in the water to the right of the wall. But no sign of the intruder appeared; the water had closed noiselessly over the now vanished figure.

"What's the matter?" asked Reade, as he stood looking, then finally flashed his light over to the other side of the wall.

"I saw——" began Hazelton. Then changed to: "I thought——er——I saw——oh, nonsense! You'll josh the life out of me!"

"Not I," Tom affirmed gravely, as a thrill of pity, for what he deemed his friend's unfortunate "nervous condition," shook him. "Tell me what you saw, Harry."

"Why, I thought I saw a big fellow——a black man, too——right behind me, arm upraised, just ready to strike me."

"Well, where is he?" Tom demanded blankly, flashing the light on either side of the narrow wall-top. "See him anywhere now, chum?"

Harry didn't. In fact, he hardly more than pretended to look. The thing that had been so real a moment before was now utterly invisible. Hazelton began to share his chum's suspicion as to the utter breakdown of his nerves and powers of vision.

"It was nothing, of course," said Harry, shamefacedly, but Tom vigorously took the other side of the question.

"See here, Harry, it must have been something," insisted Reade. "You're not dreaming, and you're not crazy. It would take either one of those conditions to make you see something that didn't really exist. No mere nervous tremor is going to make you see something as tall as a man, standing right over you, when no such thing exists."

"Well, then, where is the fellow?" Harry Hazelton demanded, helplessly, as he stared about. "There isn't any human being but ourselves in sight, either on the wall or in the water. Your light shows that."

The light did not quite show that, and could not, since the huge prowler was now swimming gently under water, some seven or eight feet from the surface.

"We'll have to solve the question before we leave here," declared Tom. "We can't have folks following us up in a ticklish place like this. Besides, Harry, I'm willing to wager that your vision——whatever it was——has some real connection with the mystery that we're going out yonder to investigate. So we'll solve the puzzle that's right here before we go forward to look at the bigger riddle that the dark now hides from us out yonder. Use your eyes, lad, an I'll do the same with mine!"

Neither Tom Reade nor Harry Hazelton are strangers to the readers of this series, nor of the series that have preceded the present one.

Tom Reade and Harry Hazelton, now engineers in charge of a big breakwater job on the Alabama gulf coast, were first introduced to our readers in the

"*Grammar School Boys Series.*" There we met them as members of that immortal band of American schoolboys known as Dick & Co. Back in the old school days Dick Prescott had been the leader of Dick & Co., though, as all our readers know, Prescott was not the sole genius of Dick & Co. Greg Holmes, Dave Darrin, Dan Dalzell and Tom and Harry had been the other members of that famous sextette of schoolboy athletes.

After reading of the doings of Dick & Co. in the "*Grammar School Boys Series,*" our readers again followed them, through the events recorded in the four volumes of the "*High School Boys Series*". Here their really brilliant work Boys Series athletes was stirringly chronicled, as along with scores of non-athletic adventures that befell them.

At the close of the high school course Dick Prescott and Greg Holmes secured appointments as cadets at the United States Military Academy at West Point. All that befell them there is duly set forth in the "*West Point Series.*" Dave Darrin and Dan Dalzell were fortunate enough to secure appointments as midshipmen in the United States Naval Academy at Annapolis, and their doings there are set forth in the "*Annapolis Series.*"

Tom Reade and Harry Hazelton, on the other hand, had felt no call to military glory. For their work in life they longed to become part of the great constructive force wielded by modern civil engineers. During the latter part of their high school work they had studied hard with ambition to become surveyors and civil engineers. In their school vacations they had sought training and experience in the offices of an engineering firm in their home town of Gridley. After being graduated from the Gridley High School, Tom and Harry had done more work in the same offices. Then, in a sudden desire for advancement, and possessed by the longing for a wider field of endeavor, Tom Reade and Harry Hazelton had secured positions as "cub engineers" on the construction work that was being done to rush a new railway, system over the Rocky Mountains in Colorado. The stern, hard work that lay before them, the many adventures in a rough wilderness, and the chain of circumstances that at last placed Tom Reade in charge of the railroad building, with Harry as first assistant engineer, are all told in the first volume of this present series, "*The Young Engineers In Colorado.*"

That great feat finished satisfactorily, the ambition of our young engineers led them further afield, as told in "*The Young Engineers in Arizona.*" A great, man-killing quicksand had to be filled in and effectively stopped from shifting. Reade & Hazelton undertook the task. Incidentally Tom came into serious, dangerous conflict with gamblers and other human birds-of-prey, who had heretofore fattened on the earnings of the railway laborers. It was a tremendously exciting time that the young engineers had in Arizona, but they at last got away with their lives and were at the same time immensely successful in their undertaking.

In "*The Young Engineers In Nevada*" we found our young friends under changed conditions. While at work in Colorado and in Arizona Tom and Harry had studied the occurrence of precious ores, and also the methods of assaying and extracting ores. Having their time wholly to themselves after finishing in Arizona the dauntless young pair went to Nevada, there to study mining at first hand. In time they located a mining claim, though there were other claimants,

6

and around this latter fact hung an extremely exciting story. Both young engineers nearly lost their lives in Nevada, and met with many strenuous situations. Their sole idea in pushing their mine forward to success was that the money so earned would enable them to further their greatest ambition; they longed to have their own engineering offices. In the end, their mine, which the young engineers had named "The Ambition," proved a success. Thereupon they left their mining partner, Jim Ferrers, in charge and went east to open their offices.

We next found the young engineers engaged to the south of the United States border. These adventures were fully set forth in the preceding volume in this series, entitled "*The Young Engineers in Mexico.*" Tom and Harry, engaged to solve some problems in a great Mexican mine, found themselves the intended tools of a pair of mine swindlers of wealth and influence. From their first realization of the swindle Tom and Harry, even in the face of threats of assured death, held out for an honest course. How they struggled to save a syndicate of American investors from being swindled out of millions of dollars was splendidly told in that fourth volume.

And now we find our young friends down at the gulf coast town of Blixton, Alabama. Here they are engaged in a kind of engineering work wholly unlike any they had hitherto undertaken. The owners of the Melliston Steamship Line, with a fleet of twenty-two freight steamships engaged in the West Indian and Central American trade, had looked in vain for suitable dock accommodations for their vessels, worth a total of more than six million dollars. In their efforts to improve their service the Melliston owners had found at Blixton a harbor that would have suited them excellently, but for one objection. The bay at Blixton was too open to shelter vessels from the severity of some of the winter gales. Up to the present time Blixton had not been used for harbor purposes. But the Melliston owners had conceived the idea that a great breakwater could be so built as to shelter the waters of the bay. They had quietly bought up most of the shore front of the little town, which had railway connection. Then they had searched about for engineers capable of building the needed breakwater. Reade & Hazelton, hearing of the project, had applied for the work. As the young men furnished most excellent recommendations from former employers they had finally secured the opportunity.

By no means was the task an easy one, as will presently be shown. It was a work that would have to be carried on in the very teeth of jealous Nature. Tom and Harry were fully aware of the great difficulties that lay before them. What they did not know was that they would presently have to contend, also, with forces set loose by wicked human minds. What started these untoward forces in operation, and how the forces worked out, will soon be seen.

Captain of a queer crew was Tom Reade, and Harry was his lieutenant. Of the laborers, seven hundred in number, some four hundred were negroes; there were also two hundred Italians and about a hundred Portuguese. Many, of each race, were skilled masons; others were but unskilled laborers. There were six foremen, all Americans, and a superintendent, also American. There were a few more Americans and two or three Scotchmen, employed as stationary engineers and in similar lines of work.

A touch of the old Arizona trouble had invaded the camp. There had recently been a pay-day, and gamblers had descended upon the camp of tents and shanties. Once more Reade had driven off the gamblers, though this time with less trouble than in Arizona. At Blixton, Tom had merely sent for the four peace officers in the town of Blixton, and had had the gamblers warned out of camp. They had gone, but there had been wrathful mutterings among many of the workmen.

The camp was a half mile back from the water's edge, on a low hillside. Here the men of the outfit were settled. There had been mutinous mutterings among some of the men, but so far there had been no open revolt.

Tom, however, who had had considerable experience in such matters, looked for some form of trouble before the smouldering excitement quieted. So did Harry.

On this dark night Tom had proposed that he and his chum take a stroll down to the shore front to see whether all were well there. Soon after leaving camp behind, the young engineers had started on a jog-trot. Just before they reached the water's edge the wind had borne to their ears the faint report of what must have been an explosion out over the waters of the gulf.

"Trouble!" Tom whispered in his chum's ear. "Most likely some of the rascals that we drove out of camp have been trying to set back our work with dynamite. If they have done so we'll teach 'em a lesson if we can catch them!"

So the young engineers had started out over their narrow retaining wall. We have seen how they had walked most of the distance when Harry had had his sudden warning of the hostile arm uplifted over his head.

"What could it have been?" demanded Tom in a low voice, as he continued to cast the light from his flash lamp out over the waters on either side of the wall.

"It must have been my nervous imagination," admitted Harry. "Whew! But it *did* seem mighty real for the moment."

"Then you're inclined, now, to believe that it was purely imagination?" pursued Tom.

"Ye——e——es, it must have been," assented Harry reluctantly.

Tom made some final casts with the light.

While they were conversing, well past the short radius of the flash lamp's glare, a massive black head bobbed up and down with the waves. Out there the huge negro who had swiftly vanished from the wall, and who had swum under water for a long distance, was indolently treading water. Wholly at home in the gulf, the man's black head blended with the darkness of the water and the blackness of the night.

"Oh, then," suggested Reade, "we may as well go along on our way. Plainly there's nothing human around here to look at but ourselves."

So they started slowly forward over the wall. Leisurely the black man swam to the wall, taking up the dogged trail again in the darkness behind the pair of young engineers.

Several minutes more of cautious walking brought Tom Reade to a startled halt.

"Look there, Harry!" uttered Reade, stopping and throwing the light ahead.

Out beyond them, not far from the end of the wall, some hundred feet of the top had been torn away. For all the young engineers could see, the foundations might have gone with the superstructure.

"Dynamite!" Tom muttered grimly. "So this is the way our newly-found enemies will fight us?"

"It won't be such a big job to repair this gap," muttered Harry calmly.

"No; but it'll take a good many dollars to pay the bills," retorted Tom.

"Well, the expense can't be charged to us, anyway," maintained Harry. "We didn't do this vandal's work, and we didn't authorize its being done."

"No; but you know why it was done, Harry," Tom continued. "It was because we drove the gamblers out of the camp, and thus made enemies for ourselves on both sides of the camp lines."

"Anyway, the company's officers can't blame us for trying to maintain proper order in the camp," Hazelton insisted stoutly.

"Not if we can stop the outrages with this one explosion, perhaps," replied Tom thoughtfully. "Yet, if there are many more tricks like this one played on the wall you'll find that the company's officers will be blaming us all the way up to the skies and down again. Big corporations are all right on enforcing morality until it hits their dividends too hard. Then you'll find that the directors will be urging us to let gambling go on again if the laborers insist on having it."

"Well, we won't have gambling in the camp, anyway," Harry retorted stubbornly. "We're simply looking after the interests of the men themselves. I wonder why they can't see it, and act like men, not fools."

"We're going to stop the gambling, and keep it stopped," Tom went on, his jaws setting firmly together. "But, Harry, we're going to have a big row on our hands, and various attempts against the company's property will be made."

"If the company's officers order us to let up on the gambling," proposed Harry, "we can resign and get out of this business altogether."

"We won't resign, and we won't knuckle down to any lot of swindlers either, Harry!" cried Tom. "Some one is fighting us, and this wreck of a sea-wall is the first proof. All right! If any one wants to fight us he shall find that we know how to fight back, and that we can hit hard. Harry, from this minute on we're after those crooks, and we'll make them realize that there's some sting to us!"

"Good enough!" cheered Hazelton. "I like that old time fight talk! But are you going to do anything to protect the wall to-night, Tom?"

"I am," announced the young chief engineer.

"What's the plan?"

"Let me think," urged Reade. "Now, I believe, I have it. We'll send one of the motor boats out here, with a foreman and four laborers. They can arm themselves with clubs and patrol the water on both sides of the wall. The 'Thomas Morton' has a small search-light on her that will be of use in keeping a close eye over the wall."

"That ought to stop the nonsense," Harry nodded. "But I don't imagine that any further efforts to destroy the wall will be made tonight, anyway."

"We'll have the night patrol out *every* night after this," Tom declared. "But I'm not so sure either, that another effort won't be made to-night, if we don't put a watch on to stop this wicked business. Harry, do you mind remaining out here while I run back and get the boat out?"

"Why should I mind?" Hazelton wanted to know.

"Well, I didn't know whether you would, or not——after seeing that imaginary something behind you."

"Don't laugh at me! I may have had a start, but you ought to be the first to know, Tom, that I haven't frozen feet."

"I do know it, Harry. You've been through too many perils to be suspected of cowardice. Well, then, I'll run back."

Tom Reade had really intended to leave the flash lamp with his chum, but he forgot to do so, and, as he jogged steadily along over the wall he threw the light ahead of him. As he got nearer shore Tom increased his jog to a brisk run.

Once, on the way, he passed the prowling negro without knowing it. That huge fellow, seeing the ray of light come steadily near him, hesitated for a few moments, then took to the water, swimming well out. After Reade had passed, the fellow swam in toward the wall.

Up on the wall climbed the negro. For a few minutes he crouched there, shaking the water from his garments. Then, cautiously, he began to crawl forward.

"Boss Reade, he done gone in," muttered the prowler. "Boss Hazelton, Ah reckon he's mah poultry!"

Harry, keeping his lone vigil away out on the narrow retaining wall, was growing sleepy. He had nearly forgotten his scare. Indeed, he was inclined to look upon it as a trick of his own brain.

CHAPTER II

THE CALL OF ONE IN TROUBLE

Once Tom Reade reached the solid land he let his long legs out into a brisk run.

With his years of practice on the Gridley High School athletic team he was not one to lose his wind readily.

So he made his way at the same speed all the way up to the camp.

"Who dar?" called a negro watchman, as Tom raced up to the outskirts of the camp.

"Reade, chief engineer," Tom called, then wheeled and made off to the right, where the more substantial barracks of the foremen stood. Superintendent Renshaw lived in a two-story barrack still farther to the right, as the guest of the young engineers.

"*Quien vive?*" (who's there?) hailed another voice, between the two barracks buildings.

"So, Nicolas, you rascal, you haven't gone to bed?" demanded Tom, halting. "What did I tell you about earlier hours?"

Nicolas was the young Mexican servant whom Tom and Harry had brought back with them from Mexico. Readers of the previous volume know all about this faithful fellow.

"You and Senor Hazelton, you waire not in bed," replied Nicolas stolidly.

"You're not expected to stay up and watch over us as if we were babies, Nicolas," spoke Tom, in a gentler voice. "You'd better turn in now."

"Senor Hazelton, where is he?" insisted Nicolas, anxiously.

"Oh, bother! Never mind where he is," Tom rejoined. "We won't either of us be in for a little while yet. But you turn in now——at once——instanter!"

Then Tom bounded over to the little porch before the foremen's barracks, where he pounded lustily on the door.

"Who's there? What's wanted?" demanded a sleepy voice from the inside.

"Is that you, Evarts?" called Reade.

"Yes, sir."

"Get on your duds and turn out as quickly as you can."

"You want me?" yawned Evarts.

"Now, see here, my man, if I didn't want you why on earth would I call you out in the middle of the night?"

"It's late," complained Evarts.

"I know it. That's why I want you to get behind yourself and push yourself," retorted the young chief engineer energetically. "Hustle!"

Twice, while he waited impatiently, Tom kicked the toe of one boot against the door to emphasize the need of haste. Other drowsy voices remonstrated.

"Hang a man who has to sleep *all* the time!" grunted Tom Reade.

After several minutes the door opened, and a lanky, loose-jointed, lantern-jawed man of some forty-odd years stepped out.

"Well, what's up, Mr. Reade?" questioned the foreman, hiding a yawn behind a bony, hairy hand.

"You are, at last, thank goodness!" Tom exclaimed. "Evarts, I want you to rout out four good men. Lift 'em to their feet and begin to throw the clothes on 'em!"

"It's pretty late to call men out of their beds, sir," mildly objected the foreman.

"No——it's early, but it can't be helped," Tom Reade retorted. "Hustle 'em out!"

"Black or white?" sleepily inquired Evarts.

"White, and Americans at that," Tom retorted. "Put none but Americans on guard tonight, Evarts! What do you suppose has happened?"

"Can't guess."

"No! You're still too sleepy. Evarts, some scoundrels have blown out a good part of our wall yonder."

"Are you joking, Mr. Reade?"

"No, sir; I am not. Dynamite must have been used. Hazelton and I heard the noise of the blast, but of course we got out there too late to catch any miscreant at the job."

Evarts, at first, was inclined to regard the news with mild disbelief, but he soon realized that something must have happened very nearly as the young chief engineer had described.

"Well, what are you standing there for?" Tom demanded, impatiently. "Are you going to wait for daylight? Get the four men out—-all Americans, mind you. *Hustle*, man!"

Evarts started away; toward the camp over to the left of them. As he did so Tom darted in another direction. Two minutes later Tom was back, piloting by one arm a man who was still engaged in rubbing the sleep out of his eyes. This was Conlon, engineer of the motor boat, "Morton."

"Where's Evarts?" Reade queried, impatiently. "Oh, Evarts! Where are you, and what are you doing?"

"Trying to get four men awake," bawled back the voice of the foreman, from the distance. "As soon as I get one man on his feet the other three have sunk back to sleep."

"Wait until I get over there then!" called Tom, striding forward. "Come along, Conlon! Don't you lag on me."

"There! Do you fellows reckon you want Mr. Reade to bump in here and shake you out?" sounded the warning voice of Evarts.

As Tom and the motor boat's engine tender reached the little, box-like shack from which Evarts's tones proceeded, four men, seated on the floor, were seen to be lacing their shoes by the dim light of a lantern.

"A nice lot you are!" called Tom crisply. "How many hours does it take you to get awake when you're called in the middle of the night?"

"This overtime warn't in the agreement," sleepily retorted one of the men.

"You're wrong there," Reade informed him, vehemently. "Overtime *is* in the agreement for every man in this camp when it's wanted of him—-from the chief engineer all along the line. Now, you men oblige me by hustling. I don't want to wait more than sixty seconds for the last man of you."

"I've a good mind to crawl back into my bunk," growled another of the men.

"All right," retorted Tom Reade, with suspicious cheerfulness. "Try it and see what kind of fireworks I carry concealed on my person. Or, just lag a little bit on me, and you'll see the same thing. Men, do you realize that there's foul play afoot out on the retaining wall? We've got to go out there in time to stop anything more happening. Now, you've got your shoes on; grab the rest of your clothing and hustle it on as we make for the beach. Come along!"

Tom fairly got behind the men and pushed them outside. They would have liked to complain, but they didn't. Some of them were larger and heavier than the chief engineer, but they knew quite well that, at sign of any trifling mutiny to-night, Reade would thrash them all.

"If any one is trying to blow up the wall, Mr. Reade, it's all your fault, anyway," ventured Evarts, as the little party started at a brisk walk for the beach. "When you've got a mixed crowd of men working for you, you shouldn't interfere too much with their amusements. Yet you would have the gamblers run out of camp just when our boys were getting ready to have some pleasant evenings."

"I'll run out any one else who attempts to bring disorderly doings into this camp," Tom retorted quietly.

12

"Then there'll be some more of your seawalls blown up," Evarts warned him gloomily.

"If such a thing happens again there'll be some men hurt, and some others breaking into prison," Tom answered with spirit. "Any evildoers that try to set themselves up in business around here will soon wish they had kept away—that's all."

"It's a bad business," insisted Evarts, wagging his head. "When you have a mixed crowd of workmen—"

"I think you've said that before," Tom broke in coolly. "To-night we're in too much of a hurry to listen to the same thing twice. Come on, men. You can go a little faster than a walk. Jog a bit—I'll show you how."

"This is pretty hard on men in the middle of the night," hinted Evarts, after the jogging had gone on for a full minute. "It ain't right to——"

"Stop it, Evarts!" Tom cut in crisply. "I don't mind a little grumbling at the right time, and I often do a bit myself, but not when I'm as rushed as I am to-night. There's the dock ahead, men—a little faster spurt now!"

Tom urged his men along to the dock. With no loss of time they tumbled aboard the "Morton," a broad, somewhat shallow, forty-foot motor boat of open construction.

"Get up and take the wheel, Evarts," Tom. directed. "Get at work on your spark, Conlon, and I'll throw the drive-wheel over for you. Some of you men cast, off!"

In a very short time the "Morton" was going "put-put-put" away from the dock.

Tom, after seeing that everything was moving satisfactorily, turned around to look at the four men huddled astern.

"Don't any of you go to sleep," he urged. "A good part of our success depends on how well you all keep awake and use your eyes and ears."

That said, Tom Reade hastened forward, stationing himself close to Evarts, who had the steering wheel.

Some of the men astern began to talk.

"Silence, if you please," Tom called softly. "Don't talk except on matters of business. We want to be able to use our ears. Conlon, make your engine a little less noisy if you can."

Now Reade had leisure to wonder how matters had gone with Harry Hazelton.

"Of course that threatening figure Harry saw behind him was an imaginary one," Tom said to himself, but he felt uneasy nevertheless.

A few moments later Reade clutched at one of Evarts's arms.

"Did you hear that, man?" the young engineer demanded.

"Hear what?" Evarts wanted to know.

"It sounded like a yell out there yonder," Tom rejoined.

"Didn't hear it, Mr. Reade."

"There it goes again!" cried Tom, leaping up. "Some one is calling my name. It must be Harry Hazelton, and he must want help. Conlon, slam it to that engine of yours!"

13

CHAPTER III
VANISHING INTO THIN AIR

Left by himself Harry had stood, at first, motionless, or nearly so. He strained his hearing in trying to detect any unusual sound of the night, since it was so dark that vision would not aid him much.

There was nothing, however, but the mournful sighing of the wind and the lapping of the waves. It seemed to Hazelton that the wind was growing gradually more brisk and the waves larger, but he was not sure of that until the water commenced splashing across his shoes. The footway on the masonry became more slippery in consequence.

"With these rocks well wet down I wouldn't care much about having to run back to the land," muttered Harry, dryly. "However, I won't have to go back on my own feet. Tom will have the boat out here, and undoubtedly he will plan to have us both taken back to shore after we get through cruising around here. We should have brought the boat out in the first place."

A night bird screamed, then flapped its wings close to Harry's face in its flight past him. The young engineer saw the moving wings for an instant; then they vanished into the black beyond.

Farther out some other kind of bird screamed. The whole situation was a weird one, but Harry was no coward, though a less courageous youth would have found the situation hard on his nerves.

Still another night bird screamed, of some species with which Hazelton was wholly unacquainted. The cry was answered by some sort of strange call from the shore.

"It's a fine thing that I'm not superstitious," laughed the young engineer to himself, "or I'd surely feel cold chills chasing each other up and down my spine."

As it was, Harry shivered slightly, though not from fear. With the increasing wind it was growing chilly out there for one who could not warm himself with exercise.

"It's a long time, or it seems so," muttered the young engineer presently. "Yet I'll wager that Tom is hustling himself and others on the very jump."

Again the call of a night bird, and once more a sound from shore seemed to answer it.

"Real birds?" wondered Hazelton, with a start of sudden curiosity. "Or have I been listening to human signals? If so, the signals can't cover any good or honest purpose."

That train of thought set him to listening more acutely than before. Yet, as no more calls reached his ears the attention of the young engineer soon began to flag.

The monotonous lapping of the waves against the stone wall, the constant splashing of water over the rocks and the steady blowing of the wind all tended to make the watcher feel drowsy.

"What on earth can be keeping good old Tom?" Harry wondered, more than once.

It would have been well, indeed, had Harry kept his eyes turned oftener toward the shore end of the wall. In that case he might more speedily have detected the wriggling, snake-like movement of the big negro moving toward him.

With great caution the huge prowler came onward, raising his head a few inches every now and then and listening. The black man's nostrils moved feverishly. He was using them, as a dog would have done, to scent any signs of alarm on the part of the human quarry that he was after.

At last Harry Hazelton turned sharply, for his own ears were attuned to the stillnesses of the western forests and his hearing was unusually acute. He had just heard a sound on the wall, not far away. Instantly the young engineer was on the alert.

Then his eyes, piercing the darkness, made out the crawling, dark form, which did not appear to be more than fifty feet away from him.

For a second or two Harry stared. But he knew there could be no snake as broad as this crawling figure appeared to be.

"Who's there?" Hazelton called quickly.

The writhing mass became still, flattening itself against the bed of rock. Hazelton was not to be deceived, however.

"Who's there?" Harry repeated. "You had better talk up, my man!"

Still no sound. Harry started forward to investigate. His foot touched against a good sized fragment of rock left there by one of the masons.

Without delay Harry reached down, picking up the rock, which was rather more than half as large as his head.

Holding this in his right hand Harry advanced with still more confidence, for he felt himself to be armed. Hazelton had been a clever pitcher in his high school days and knew that he could make this fragment of rock land pretty close to where he wanted it to go.

"Who are you?" demanded Hazelton, once more, as he stepped cautiously forward. "No use in your keeping silent, my man. I see you and know that you're there. Moreover, I'm going to drag the truth out of you as to what you're doing out here on the wall at this hour of the night—and to-night of all nights."

Still no answer; Harry went steadily forward, until he was within a dozen feet of the head of the flattened brute in human guise. Hazelton could now see every line of his adversary plainly, though he could not make out the fellow's face.

"You'd better get up and talk," warned Harry, poising the rock fragment for a throw. "If you don't you'll cast all the more suspicion upon yourself. For the last time, my man, who are you and what are you doing here?"

The huge black figure might have been a log for all the answer that came forth.

"All right, then; it's your own fault," Harry Hazelton continued calmly. "As you won't speak I'm going to crack the nut for myself. Your head will be the nut, and this rock I have in my hand shall be the hammer. I'm going to slam this rock on your head with all the force I've got, and I'm a good, straight thrower."

Yet, though Hazelton spoke with such confidence, he was far from meaning all he said. In the first place, he had no legal right, under the circumstances, to go as close to murder as it might be for him to throw the rock at the rascal's head.

15

Moreover, Harry would hardly have exercised such a legal right, had he possessed it, without the strongest provocation.

From the black prowler came a sudden, fierce snort. It sounded altogether like defiance.

"Ho——ho! You're finding your voice, are you, my man?" Hazelton jeered. "Then talk up in time to save yourself!"

Instead the huge black man began to writhe forward.

"Stop that!" ordered Harry dangerously. He did not retreat from the writhing human thing, but he took better aim, noting that the black man was hatless and that his head offered a fair mark. "You're going to get hurt in just about a second more," he added.

Uttering another snort the bulky black sprang to his feet with surprising agility in one of his great size.

Harry now let his right hand fall back quickly. He was poising for the throw in earnest, for there could no longer be any doubt that the stranger was planning a deadly assault.

"Take it, then, since you want it!" snapped out Harry Hazelton. The fragment of rock left his hand, propelled with force and directed with accurate aim at the negro's face.

But the crafty black dodged just in time, at the same instant throwing up his hands.

Harry gasped as he saw his unknown assailant deftly catch the rock fragment as though it had been a base ball.

"Ha, ha! Ho, ho!" jeered the black, in a hoarse, rumbling voice.

He threw back his hand, gathering impetus for the cast. Hazelton could do nothing but throw himself on the defensive, planning to duplicate the black man's catch.

Then the stone came——but it did not go high, instead, by a jerk of his wrist, the negro hurled it at Harry's right foot.

That granite-like fragment struck Hazelton's foot with full force.

"You——you scoundrel!" groaned Harry, in an all but admiring gasp.

Like a flash he bent over, snatching up the fragment for his own use.

"Now, I'll slam you into the middle of the Gulf of Mexico!" cried the young engineer, vengefully, as he tried to straighten up.

A groan escaped him. His injured foot was paining him more than he had expected.

"Ha, ha! Ho, ho!" harshly jeered this mysterious, evil creature. The black man had halted as Harry prepared to throw, but he showed no sign of hesitation. Though he stood still, he thrust his repulsive, leering face forward, as though to offer that face as the best mark.

Harry found that he could not stand straight——the pain in his injured foot was now too intense.

"Get back with you!" ordered Harry. "Get back if you don't want a heap worse than you gave me."

"Ha, ha! Ho, ho!" came the sneering laugh. Then the stranger reached out his hands as though to seize the youth.

16

"I guess I'll have to do it——though not because I really want to hurt you!" muttered Harry ruefully.

"Ha, ha! Ho, ho!"

There could be no question that the unknown was merely playing with him. Little as he liked to make the ugly throw Harry knew that he had to do it. When Hazelton had anything to do he believed in doing it well. So, putting all possible force into his throw, Harry let the rock fragment fly, and this time he was sure that his enemy would not be able to dodge in time.

Nor did the black man make any seeming effort to dodge.

Bump! Squarely in the black face the rock landed. Harry heard the sound and felt ill within himself. Yet the black man did not stagger. With a contemptuous snort he kicked the fragment of rock into the water as it landed at his feet.

"Ha, ha! Ho, ho!"

For the first time Harry Hazelton felt positively dismayed. He saw the long, massive arms moving, looking like a powerful ape's arms. There could be no doubt that the unknown was ready for a spring.

Harry did not retreat. Where could he run to? Only a few yards could he go out towards the end of the wall. Then, if he wished to continue his flight he could only take to the water.

Only a glance was needed at the bulky, powerful frame of the unknown to make it appear certain that the latter could swim two rods to the young engineer's one.

Harry decided instantly to stand his ground and to make the most valiant fight possible on so slippery a footing as that presented by the top of the retaining wall.

"Ha, ha! Ho, ho!"

It was as though the black unknown sought to terrify his intended victim with his repetitions of that harsh, discordant laugh. Harry braced himself and waited.

Then, off shoreward, came the sound of "put-put-put." The motor boat, "Morton," was putting out at last.

"If I can keep this fellow busy for a few minutes, I can have all the help I want," flashed through Hazelton's mind. So he opened his mouth, raising his voice in a long, pent-up hail.

"R e——e——e a d e! To——o——o——om R e a d e! Quick! Hazelton!"

"Ha, ha!" jeered the unknown black.

Then, suddenly, he leaped——not unexpectedly, however, for Harry had been watching, cat-like.

The unknown threw out his arms, seeking to wrap them around Hazelton.

Not in vain had Harry been trained, season after season, on the athletic ground of one of the best high school elevens in the United States.

As the fellow leaped at him Harry crouched lower and went straight at his opponent.

Powerful as the stranger was he was no football player. Harry "tackled" him in the neatest possible way, then strove to rise with this great human being.

In the first instant it seemed to the young engineer as though he were trying to lift a mountain. His back felt as though it were snapping under a giant's task.

Yet, but for one fact, Hazelton would have risen with his man, and would have hurled the mysterious one over into the waters of the gulf.

Just in the instant of victory Harry's injured right foot gave out under him. With a stifled groan he sank down just as he threw his opponent.

The black, instead of going into the water, landed hard on his back on the top of the wall. He was up again, however, before Hazelton could repress the pain in his foot and leap at the wretch.

"Ha, ha! Ho, ho!" came the tantalizing challenge.

"Put-put-put!" sounded over the water, coming nearer all the time.

"Re——e——e——e a d e! T o m R e a d e! Help——quick!" yelled Harry, lustily.

This, doubtless, was the first call that Tom, at the bow of the motor boat, thought he heard.

Uttering a snort, this time, instead of the laugh, the black sprang at his intended prey. Their heads met, with considerable force. Then, with a wild chuckle, the black wound his apelike arms around the young engineer.

"Reade! Tom Reade! Reade!" bellowed Hazelton lustily, as he tried desperately to free himself from the crushing embrace of the other.

* * * * *

Over the waters came the penetrating beam of a small search-light. The "Morton" was coming nearer all the time, but the ray did not yet reach with any great clearness the point where Harry Hazelton had been fighting for his life against his strange foe in the black night.

"Keep parallel with the wall, Evarts," Tom ordered, crisply. "Conlon, are you pushing the engines for all it's worth?"

"Yes, sir," came from the engine-tender. "This old craft isn't good for quite seven miles' an hour, anyway."

"There! Now I've picked up the part of the wall where there isn't any wall in sight just now," said Tom, wincing over his own bull. "Hazelton ought to be just this side of there."

"There's no one near the breach," replied Evarts.

"So I see," Reade admitted, in a tone of worriment. "Oh, well, Harry isn't such an infant as to be wiped out all in one moment."

"Where is Mr. Hazelton then?" inquired Evarts, as Tom swung the arc of the searchlight in broad curves.

"Great Scott! I wish I knew!" gasped Reade, his perplexity and his anxiety growing with every second. "There appears to be no one on top of the wall."

Evarts ran in within a few feet of the wall, on the shore-side of the breach.

"Shall I land you there, sir?" questioned the foreman.

"Presently," Tom nodded. "But now, back out a few feet and swing the boat's nose around so that I can make a search with this light." Evarts obeyed the order. Despite the smallness of the light, Reade was able to send the searching beam of light back nearly one-half of the way to shore. Nowhere was there any human being visible on the wall.

"Harry! Hazelton!" bawled Tom, with all the power in his lungs.

There was no answer.

18

"Jupiter! You'll have to land me, I reckon," quaked Tom Reade. "Drive her nose in——gently. I'll be ready to jump."

"Be careful how you *do* jump," warned Evarts. "It's mighty slippery on that wall tonight."

Tom poised himself as the boat moved in close. Then he took a light leap, landing safely.

Here the young chief engineer again brought his pocket flash lamp into play. Closely he scanned the top of the wall all around where he knew he had left his chum.

But Harry was nowhere to be seen, nor, on the wet wall, could Tom find any signs of a scuffle, or any other sign that gave him a clue.

"Evarts, this is mighty mysterious!" groaned the young chief.

"Unless——" hinted the foreman.

"Unless what?"

"Perhaps Mr. Hazelton ran along the walltop to the shore."

"He'd have hailed us, then, in passing, wouldn't he?" choked Tom Reade. "Besides, I had the light playing on this wall most of the way. If he had run back we would have seen him, even if he hadn't hailed. And he couldn't have run farther out to seaward. Evarts, I'm downright worried."

Tom Reade might indeed well be worried over the grewsome mysteries of this night of evil deeds.

CHAPTER IV

SOME ONE CALLS AGAIN

Half an hour later Tom Reade leaped ashore at the little pier.

"My orders, Mr. Reade."

"They're brief and concise," Tom rejoined. "You're to cruise the length of the wall, especially farther out from shore. Use your searchlight freely. Keep the wall so guarded that no rascal can slip out there, either over the wall or by boat, and do any damage. Mr. Evarts, the safety of the wall until daylight is your whole charge."

"Very good, sir. But I'm sure that nothing more will happen to the wall."

"If anything does it will be up to you, Mr. Evarts," Tom assured him grimly. "I'll hold you responsible."

"I won't let anything happen, Mr. Reade. And I hope you find Mr. Hazelton all right."

"He may be up at camp," Tom answered, though in his heart he did not believe it.

Had Harry escaped whatever danger had menaced him, Tom knew very well that his chum, after appealing for help, would by some means have signaled his subsequent safety.

However, Tom started toward camp at a run. He was wholly mystified. The search in the neighborhood of the breach in the wall had been continued until its hopelessness had been fully demonstrated. The search had also been continued over the water, for a possible clue to the mystery.

Though Tom ran, he felt himself choking, stifling. Despite all his efforts to cheer himself the young chief engineer felt certain that his chum had

19

mysteriously met his fate, and that brave, dependable Harry Hazelton was no more.

Yet how could he have vanished so completely, and what possibly could have happened to his assailant or assailants?

"It'll be an awful night, until daylight," Tom groaned inwardly, as he ran. "At daylight, of course, we can make a far better search, especially over the water. But in the hours that must elapse—! It's going to be a tough period of waiting!"

Arrived at camp, Tom made straight for his own barracks, letting himself in with a latch-key as soon as he could control his shaking hand sufficiently to use the key.

Tom bounded straight for the bed-room of the superintendent, at the rear of the little building.

"Mr. Renshaw!" shouted the young chief, throwing open the bed-room door.

The barrack was lighted by electricity. Tom threw on the light, then wheeled toward the bed, to find the superintendent sitting up, revolver in hand.

"Oh, it's you, is it?" gasped the superintendent. "Mr. Reade, in my stupor from being aroused I was just on the point of shooting you for a burglar. It's awful!"

"You ought to throw that revolver to the bottom of the gulf," Tom rasped out.

"Not much!" retorted the superintendent. "Handling as mixed a crew as we have on this work I wouldn't think of going about unarmed. And you ought to go armed, too, Mr. Reade."

"Bosh!" uttered Tom. He had a well-known objection to carrying a pistol. Reade always maintained that a pistol-carrying man was a coward. A coward is one who is afraid, and the man who is not afraid has no reason to carry a weapon.

"Renshaw," added Tom, "there's just one circumstance in which I would carry a pistol—and that is, if I were carrying large sums of other people's money. If I were a pay-master, or a bank messenger, I'd carry a pistol, but under no other circumstances, outside of military service, would I carry a weapon. But—-are you thoroughly awake, now?"

"Yes, sir."

"Then, Mr. Renshaw, get up and hide that pistol somewhere. While you're about it, listen to me. Some scoundrel has blown out a large portion of our retaining wall to-night. I left Hazelton on guard at the point and came ashore to get out the motor boat, 'Morton.' Before I could return I heard Hazelton's call for help, and—-he has disappeared! There's wicked work on hand to-night. You'll have to get up and help me. Be quick with your dressing. We've work to do to-night, and all of it is man's work."

Tom hastily added such other particulars as were needed. Renshaw, while he dressed hurriedly, listened with a horror that he took no pains to conceal.

"Evarts claims that it's revenge work, on the part of some of our men, because Hazelton and I stopped gambling in the camp," Tom continued.

"It might be," Renshaw admitted thoughtfully. "But to me it seems that there must be a lot more behind the whole terrible matter."

"That's the way it strikes me, too," Tom nodded. "However, you're dressed, so now we can hurry out and get busy."

20

"What shall we do first?" Superintendent Renshaw inquired.

"That's what I've been thinking over while you were dressing," Tom replied. "Of course the one thing of real importance is to find Hazelton."

"Killed, beyond a doubt," replied the older man.

"I refuse to believe it," Tom retorted. "There's a mystery in his fate, but I simply won't believe that Harry has been killed."

"Then why didn't you hear from him further?"

"That's the mystery."

Tom had shaped their course for the barracks occupied by the foremen. He bounded upon the little porch and began to hammer on the door with both fists.

"Turn out, everybody!" Tom bellowed. "Every foreman is on duty to-night. Show a light, and let us in as soon as you can."

Some one was heard stirring. Then Dill, one of the foremen, admitted the callers.

"Are all the others up?" Reade asked, sharply.

"Yes, sir."

"Good! Tell your associates to finish dressing as quickly as possible and to meet me in the office."

"The office" was a little room just inside the entrance to the building. It was a room where the foremen sat and chatted in the evenings.

"Put a double-hustle on, everyone," Tom called after Dill.

"Yes, sir."

Barely three minutes had passed when all of the six remaining foremen had assembled. Tom plunged instantly into a brief account of what had happened.

"It seems to me, sir—" Dill began.

"Keep it to yourself, then, if you please," Tom interrupted him gently. "We haven't any time for opinions to-night. What we want is swift, intelligent work, and a lot of it."

Tom thereupon gave each man his directions.

"Now, each of you go to your own gangs in the camp," he added. "Wake what men you need and put 'em to work. If any of the men object to being taken from their cots in the night, just lift them out. Don't stand any nonsense. Let each foreman make it his business to know just what the men under him are doing."

One foreman was to take men with lanterns and go out carefully over every foot of the seawall. Another was to organize a beach patrol. Still another, with but two men, was to go into the town of Blixton and see if any tidings of Hazelton could be obtained there. To one foreman fell the task of searching carefully through camp before going to other work assigned to him.

"Now, get to work, all of you," Tom ordered. "As an extra inducement you can tell your men that the one who finds Hazelton, whether dead or alive, shall have a reward of one hundred dollars. Remember the watchword for to-night, which is, 'hustle!'"

In all, some sixty men were pulled from their cots. Tom, having given the orders, walked down to the beach with his superintendent.

"You've covered everything that's possible, I think, Mr. Reade," commented the foreman.

21

"I think I have. But there won't be any rest for any one until we have found Hazelton."

"Are you going to have the water dragged?"

"Not before daylight——perhaps not then," Reade replied. "I can't bring myself to believe that Harry was thrown into the water and that he drowned there."

"It'll take the chief a day or two to realize that," sighed the superintendent to himself. "Yet that is exactly what has happened. The chief won't believe it, though, until the body is found."

Down on the beach there was really nothing for Tom and his head man to do after the arrival of the foremen and their gangs. Everything went ahead in an orderly manner.

"I don't suppose you could get any rest, under the circumstances, Mr. Reade," hinted the superintendent, "yet that is just what you are going to need."

"Rest?" echoed Tom, gazing at the man, in a strange, wide-eyed way, while a grim smile flickered around the corners of his mouth. "What have rest and I to do with each other just now?"

"Yet there's nothing you can do here."

"I am here, anyway," Reade retorted. "I'm on the spot——that's something."

"Let me run back to the house and get you some blankets," urged the superintendent. "Then you can lie down on the sand and rest. Of course I know you can't sleep at present."

"It is not necessary go back," volunteered a voice behind them. "I have the blankets."

"Nicolas!" gasped Tom, in surprise. "How did you know I was here?"

"I wake up when you talk to Meester Renshaw," replied the Mexican simply. "I listen. I know, now——poor Senor Hazelton!"

Nicolas's voice broke, and, as he stepped closer, Tom beheld some large tears trickling down the little Mexican's face.

"Nicolas, you're a good fellow!" cried Tom, impulsively, "but I don't want the blankets. Spread them on the sand, then lie down on them yourself until I need you."

"What——me? I lie down?" demanded Nicolas. "No, no! That impossible is. I must walk, walk! Me? I am like the caged panther to-night. I want nothing but find the enemy who have hurt Senor Hazelton. Then I jump on the back of that enemy!"

Saying which Nicolas saluted, and, as became his position of servant, fell back some yards. But first he had dropped the blankets to the beach.

The light of lanterns showed that the men of one gang were searching thoroughly all along the top of the wall. Once in a while a man belonging to the beach patrol passed the chief engineer and the superintendent, reporting only that no signs of Harry had been found.

An hour thus passed. Then, from over the water, as the lantern-bearing searchers were returning, a dull explosion boomed across the water.

"Great Scott!" quivered Tom. "There they go at it again, Mr. Renshaw! Another section of the retaining wall has gone——blown up!"

CHAPTER V

WANTED—-DAYLIGHT AND DIVERS

In a trice the foreman of the gang on the wall wheeled his men about, running them out seaward toward the scene of the latest explosion. That much was plain from the twinkling of the rapidly-moving lanterns.

"Come on, Renshaw!" Tom shouted. "You, too, Nicolas. You can pull an oar."

Reade was already racing out on to the small dock. He all but threw himself into a rowboat that lay tied alongside.

"Cast off and get in," Tom ordered his companions, as he pushed out a pair of oars. "Nicolas, you're also good with a pair of oars. Mr. Renshaw, you take the tiller. Inform me instantly when you see the first gleam of the 'Morton's' search-light. Evarts ought to have caught the scoundrels this time. Evidently he's been cruising softly without showing a light."

Mr. Renshaw gathered up the tiller ropes as Tom pushed off from the dock. Then the chief engineer addressed himself to the task of rowing. His firm muscles, working at their best, shot the little craft ahead. Nicolas, at the bow oars, did his best to keep up with his chief in the matter of rowing, though the Mexican was neither an oarsman nor an athlete.

"Don't you make out the motor boat's lights yet?" Tom asked impatiently, after the first long spurt of rowing.

"Not yet, sir," replied the superintendent. "I shan't miss the light when it shows."

A few minutes later the superintendent announced in a low voice:

"There's some craft, motionless, just a bit ahead."

Tom, without stopping his work at the oars, turned enough to glance forward.

"Why, it's——it's the 'Morton'!" he gasped.

"I believe it is," declared the superintendent, staring keenly at the nearly shapeless black mass ahead.

Tom, with his jaws set close, bent harder than ever at the oars.

"Senor!" wailed Nicolas, gaspingly. "If you do not go more easily I shall expire for lack of breath. I cannot keep up with you."

Reade fell into a slower, stronger stroke.

"Drop the oars any time you want to, Nicolas," Reade urged. "There won't be much more rowing to do, anyway."

Presently Tom himself rested on his oars, as the boat, moving under its own headway, approached the motor boat.

"Going to board her on the quarter?" the superintendent asked.

"No; by the bow," Tom answered. "Let go the tiller ropes. I'll pull alongside."

As they started to pass the boat a sound reached them that made Reade grow wild with anger. Snore after snore, from five busy sleepers!

Tom pulled softly up to the bow.

"There's the anchor cable!" snorted Tom, Pointing to a rope that ran from the bow of the "Morton" down into the water. "Did you ever see more wicked neglect of important duty? And not even a lantern out to mark her berth! Get aboard, Mr. Renshaw, and go aft to start the engine. Nicolas, you take this boat astern and make fast. Don't wake the sleepers——poor, tired shirkers!"

Tom, in utter disgust, leaped aboard the boat at the bow. There, behind the wheel, Evarts lay on the floor of the boat, his rolled-up coat serving as a pillow.

Almost noiselessly Tom hauled up the light anchor. Then he stood by the wheel.

"All ready at the engine, Mr. Reade!" called the superintendent, softly.

"Let her go," Tom returned, "as soon as Nicolas boards."

The Mexican was quickly aboard, after having made the rowboat's painter fast.

"Headway!" announced Renshaw, throwing over the drive-wheel of the engine.

"Put-put-put!" sputtered the motor. Then the "Morton" began really to move. With the first real throb of the engine the electric running lights gleamed out.

Aft Conlon began to stir. Then he opened his eyes.

"What——" he began.

"Silence!" commanded Mr. Renshaw.

"Tell me who's at the wheel?" Conlon begged.

"Mr. Reade," replied the superintendent, dryly. "Now, keep still!"

"Whew——-ew——-ew!" whistled Conlon, in dire dismay. Then he sank back, watching the engine with moody eyes. The other three men aft still slept.

Presently Tom, in shifting his position, touched one foot lightly against the foreman's head. Evarts half-awoke, then realized that the boat was moving.

"Who started this craft against my orders?" he drowsily demanded, as he sat up.

"I did," Tom retorted witheringly, "though I didn't hear your orders to the contrary."

"You——Mr. Reade?" gasped the foreman, leaping to his feet.

"Yes——and a fine fellow you are to trust!" Tom rejoined. "I leave you with very definite orders, and you go to sleep. Then there's another explosion out on the wall and you sleep right along."

"Another explosion?" blurted Evarts, rubbing his eyes with his fists.
"Here, let me have that wheel, sir. I'll have you out there quick!"

"You've nothing more to do here," Tom answered, dryly, without yielding the wheel.

"What do you mean by that?" Evarts cried quickly.

"Can't you guess?" wondered Reade.

"Mr. Reade means," said Conlon, who had come forward, "that we're fired—— discharged."

"Nonsense!" protested Evarts.

"Conlon has guessed rightly, as far as you're concerned," Tom continued. "To-morrow, Evarts, you go to Mr. Renshaw and get your pay. As for you, Conlon, you're not discharged this time. Evarts admitted himself that it was he who gave positive orders to tie the boat up at anchor. You were under his orders, so I can't hold you responsible. Are you wide awake, now?"

"Yes, sir," answered Conlon meekly.

"Then go back and attend to your engine. Look sharp for hail or bell."

"I guess you'll find you can't quite get along without me," argued Evarts moodily. "You'll find that you need me to manage some of the men you've got."

"You're through with this job, as I just did you the honor to inform you," Tom responded quietly. "To-morrow Mr. Renshaw will pay you off up to date."

"If I'm bounced, then you'll pay me for the balance of the month, anyway!" snarled the foreman defiantly. "You can't drop me without notice like that."

"You'll be paid to date only," Tom retorted. "You've been discharged for wilful and serious neglect of duty, and you're not entitled to pay for the balance of the month."

"All right, then," retorted the other hotly. "I'll collect my money through the courts. I'll show you!"

"Just as you please," Reade replied indifferently. "But I imagine any court will consider seven dollars a day pretty large pay for a man who goes to sleep on duty."

"See here, I'll——"

"You'll keep quiet, Evarts, or you'll go overboard," Reade interrupted significantly. "I happen to know that you can swim, so I won't be bothered with you here if you insist on making a nuisance of yourself."

Mr. Renshaw, having been relieved at the engine, now came forward.

"Mr. Renshaw," directed the young chief engineer, "as soon after daylight as it is convenient for you you'll pay Evarts off in full to date and let him go. He threatens to sue if he is not paid to the end of the month, but if he wants to we'll let the courts do our worrying."

"All right, sir," nodded the superintendent.

Evarts had dropped into a seat just forward of the engine. He sat there, regarding Tom Reade with a baleful look of hate.

"You're a success, all right, at one thing, and that's making enemies," muttered the discharged foreman under his breath.

Besides attending to the wheel Tom now reached out with one hand and switched on the search-light, which he manipulated with one hand. Shortly he found the spot where the portion of the wall had been blown away by the first explosion. A hundred and fifty yards farther out he beheld the work of the second explosion. Some seventy-five yards in length was the new open space, where at least as much of the retaining wall as was visible above the water had been blown out.

"Slow down, Cordon," ordered Tom. "All we want is headway."

"All right, sir."

Tom drifted in within a few feet of the former site of the retaining wall. The "Morton" moved slowly by, Tom, by the aid of the searchlight, noting the extent of the disaster.

"Get back aft, Evarts," ordered the young engineer, turning and beholding the late foreman. "We don't want you here."

For a moment or two it looked as though Evarts would refuse. Then, with a growl, he rose and picked his way aft. By this time the other men who had been in his gang were awake. They regarded their former foreman with no great display of sympathy.

"I'll confess I'm mystified," muttered Tom, watching the scene of the latest explosion for some minutes after the engine had been stopped. "When daylight

25

comes and we can use the divers we ought to know a bit more about how such a big blast is worked in the dead of night when the scoundrels ought to make noise enough to be heard. It must have been a series of connected blasts, all touched off at the same moment, Mr. Renshaw, but even such a series is by no means easy to lay. And then the blasts have to be drilled for, and then tamped."

"As you say, sir," replied the superintendent, "a much clearer idea can be formed when we have daylight and the divers."

Tom held his watch to one side of the searchlight.

"Nearly two hours yet until daylight, Mr. Renshaw," he announced. "And, of course, it will be two or three hours after daylight before we can get the divers at work. A fearful length of time to wait!"

"You'd better go back to the shore, sir," urged the superintendent.

"Not while this boat needs to be run," objected Reade. "For the rest of the night I want a man here whom I can trust."

"Will you trust me with the boat?" proposed the superintendent.

"Why, of course!"

"Then let me run back to the dock and put you ashore, Mr. Reade. After that I'll come out here and patrol along the wall until broad daylight."

That was accordingly done. The "Morton" lay alongside the dock, and Nicolas instantly busied himself with casting off the rowboat and making her fast to the pier instead.

Evarts sullenly remained in the boat.

"Come on, Evarts," spoke Tom quietly.

"Mr. Reade," expostulated the late foreman, "I'm not going to be thrown out of my job like this."

"Which especial way of being thrown out do you prefer then?" Tom queried, dryly.

"I'm not going to be put out of my job until I've had at least one good talk with you," insisted the foreman.

"I'm afraid the time has passed for talking with you," Reade responded, turning toward the shore. "You lost a great chance, to-night, to serve the company with distinction, and your negligence cost the company a lot of money through the second explosion. Are you coming out of that boat——or shall I come back after you?"

Evarts rose, with a surly air. He stepped slowly ashore, after which one of the crew cast off. The engine began to move, and the "Morton" started back to her post.

"Oh, you feel fine and important, just at this minute!" grumbled the discharged foreman, under his breath, glaring wickedly at the broad back of the young chief engineer. "But I'll do something to take the importance out of you before very long, Tom Reade!"

Truth to tell, Tom, though he was still alert to the interests of his employers, felt anything but important. The thought of Harry Hazelton's unknown fate caused a great, choking lump in his throat as Reade stepped from the pier to land.

CHAPTER VI

MR. BASCOMB IS PEEVISH

At the first blush of dawn Tom despatched the tireless Nicolas to Blixton to notify the police of the explosions and of the disappearance of Harry Hazelton.

Two men in blue, wearing stars on their coats, came over within an hour, walked about and looked wise until noon. They discovered nothing whatever, and their theories did not strike Reade as being worthy of attention.

As soon as possible the divers were sent down at the two wrecked parts of the retaining wall. These men reported that the breaches extended ten feet beneath the surface at some points; only eight feet at other points. The foundations of the walls were reported as being secure. Then Tom, under the directions of two divers, put on a diver's suit and went down himself, for the first time in his life. After some two hours, with frequent ascents to the surface, the young chief engineer had satisfied himself that the foundations were secure. Then he did some rapid figuring.

"The loss will not exceed eight thousand dollars——the cost of rebuilding the missing parts of the walls," Reade informed Superintendent Renshaw.

"Only eight thousand dollars!" whistled the superintendent.

"Well, that figure isn't anywhere nearly as high as I feared it might be," Tom pursued.

"But it will strike the directors of the Melliston Company as being pretty big for an extra bill," muttered Renshaw. "Especially, since——"

The superintendent paused.

"You were going to say," smiled Tom, wanly, "since the loss wouldn't have happened if I hadn't kicked the gamblers out of camp."

"That's about the size of it, Mr. Reade," nodded Renshaw. "Directors of big companies are less interested in moral reforms than in dividends. They're likely to make a big kick over what your crusade has cost them already, even if it costs them no more."

"We'll see to it that it doesn't cost them any more," Tom retorted. "Every night we'll watch that sea wall the way a mother does a sick baby. There'll be no more explosions. As to the directors kicking over the present expense, they'll have a prompt chance to do it. As soon as the telegraph office in Blixton was open this morning I wired the president of the company. Now, I'm going ashore. I can't do anything out here to help you, can I?"

"Nothing," replied Renshaw. "If I didn't know how foolish the advice would sound, Mr. Reade, I'd urge you to take a nap."

"I'll take a nap when I find it impossible to keep my eyes open any longer," Tom compromised. "For the next few hours——work and lots of it."

As yet no effort had been made to repair the breaches in the wall. The different gangs were working that day in nearer shore. The divers, gathered on a scow, were now waiting for the "Morton" to convey them back to shore. Reade decided to go with them.

"Twenty minutes to two," murmured Tom to himself, glancing at his watch as the "Morton" went laboriously back over the dancing, glinting waves. "There's a train due at Blixton at 1:30. By the time I get back to the house I ought to find one or more officials of the company impatiently waiting to jump on my devoted neck."

Nor was Tom disappointed in this expectation. Pacing up and down on the porch of the house occupied by the engineers and superintendent was George C. Bascomb, president of the Melliston Company. Behind him stood Nicolas, respectfully eager to do anything he could for the comfort of the great man.

"Ah, there you are, Reade," called President Bascomb in an irritated tone, as he caught sight of the young engineer striding forward. "Now, what's all this row that you wired us about?"

"Will you come down to the water, and go out with me to look at the damage, sir?" asked Tom, as he took the president's reluctantly offered hand.

"No," grunted Mr. Bascomb. "Let me hear the story first. Come inside and tell me about it."

"Our friend is not quite so gracious as he has been on former meetings," thought Tom, as he led the way inside. "I wonder if he is going to get cranky?"

Inside was a little office room, as in the foremen's barracks.

"Any decent cigars here?" questioned Mr. Bascomb, after exploring his own pockets and finding them innocent of tobacco.

"No, sir," Tom answered. "No one here smokes."

"I've got to have a cigar," the president of the company insisted.

"Then, sir, if you'll give Nicolas your orders, he'll run over to Blixton and get you what you want."

The Mexican departed in haste on the errand.

"Now, first of all, Reade," began the president, "I am disgusted at learning of one fool mistake that you've made."

"What is that, sir?" Tom asked, coloring.

"I've just learned that you discharged Evarts——one of our best and most useful men."

"I did discharge him, sir," Reade admitted.

"Take him back, at once."

"I'm sorry, sir, but I can't do it. He——"

"I don't think you quite understand," broke in Mr. Bascomb coldly. "I directed you to take Mr. Evarts back on this work."

"I was about to tell you, sir, why I can't do anything of the sort. I——"

"Stop right there, Reade," ordered President Bascomb, in his most aggressive, bullying manner. "The first point that we have to settle is that Evarts must come back on the pay-roll and have his old position. Be good enough to let that proposition sink in before we take up the second."

"I am very sorry, sir," Tom murmured respectfully, "but I can't and won't have Evarts back here. I won't have him around the work at all. Now what is the second proposition, sir?"

As Tom spoke he looked straight into Mr. Bascomb's eyes. The other glared at him unbelievingly but angrily.

"Young man, you don't appear to understand that I am president and head of the Melliston Company."

"I quite understand it, sir," Reade answered. "At the same time I am chief engineer here, and I am committed to building the breakwater and dredging out the enclosed bay or harbor, all within a certain fixed appropriation. In order to keep my part of the bargain I must have men with me on whom I can depend to the fullest limit. Evarts isn't such a man and I won't have him on the work again."

"He'll go on the pay-roll, anyway," snorted Mr. Bascomb.

"I can't help what you may see fit to pay him, Mr. Bascomb, provided you pay him somewhere else. But the fellow can't go on the pay-roll here for the simple reason that he wouldn't be allowed to visit this construction camp for the purpose of getting his money. Mr. Bascomb, I am not trying to ride a high horse. I recognize that you are president of the company, and that I must take all reasonable orders from you and carry them out to the letter. Yet I can't take any orders that would simply hinder my work and damage my reputation as an engineer. Evarts can't come back into this camp as long as I am in charge here."

"We'll take that up again presently," returned Mr. Bascomb, with an air of ruffled dignity. "Now, there's another matter that we must discuss. I know what has been done in the way of great damage to the retaining wall. I also know that this damage came through enmity that you stirred up by drumming certain parties out of this camp."

"You refer, sir, I take it, to my act in having Blixton police officers come in here and chase out some gamblers who had come here for the purpose of winning the money of the workmen?"

"That's it," nodded Bascomb. "In that matter you went too far——altogether too far!"

"I'm afraid I don't understand you, sir."

"You mean, Reade, that you don't want to understand me," snapped the president. "You admit having chased out the gamblers, don't you?"

"Of course, I admit it, sir."

"That was a bad move. In the future, Reade, you will not interfere with any forms of amusement that the men may select for themselves in their evening hours."

Tom stared at the speaker in undisguised amazement.

"But, Mr. Bascomb, the men are shamelessly robbed by the sharpers who come here to gamble with them."

"That's the men's own affair," scoffed the president. "Anyway, they have a right to pitch away their wages if they want to. Reade, when you're as old as I am you will understand that workmen who throw away their money make the best workmen. They never have any savings, hence they must make every effort to keep their jobs. A workman with savings becomes too independent."

"I am certain you have seen more of the world than I have, Mr. Bascomb," Reade replied, respectfully. "At the same time I can't agree with you on the point you have just stated. A workman with a bank account has always a greater amount of self-respect, and a man who has self-respect is bound to make a good citizen and a good workman. But there are still other reasons why I had the gamblers chased out. Gambling here in the camp would always create a great deal of disorder. Disorder destroys discipline, and a camp like this, in order to give the best results in the way of work, must have discipline. Moreover, the men, when gambling, remain up until all hours of the night. A man who has been up most of the night can't give an honest day's work in return for his wages. Unless the men get their sleep and are kept in good condition we can't get the work out of them that we have a right to expect."

"The right man can *drive* workmen," declared Mr. Bascomb, with emphasis. "You'll have to drive your men. Get all the work out of them, but drop at once this foolish policy of interfering with what they do after the whistle blows. We can't have any more of this nonsense. It costs too much. By the way, how much will it cost to repair the damage to the retaining walls?"

"About eight thousand dollars, sir, if my first figuring was correct," was Reade's answer.

"Eight thousand dollars!" scowled President Bascomb. "Now, Reade, doesn't that amount of wanton, revengeful mischief teach you the folly of trying to regulate camp life outside of working hours?"

"I'm afraid it doesn't, sir."

"Then you must be a fool, Reade!"

"Thank you, sir. I will add that you're not the first man who has suspected it."

"You will, therefore, Reade," continued Mr. Bascomb, with his grandest air of authority, "cause it to become known throughout the camp that you are not going to interfere any further with any form of amusement that is brought to the camp evenings by outsiders."

"Is that proposition number two, sir?" queried the young chief engineer.

"It is."

"Then please don't misunderstand me, sir," Reade begged, respectfully, "but it is declined, as is proposition number one."

"Do you mean to say that you are going to go on with your fool way of doing things?"

"Yes, sir—until I am convinced that it is a fool way."

"But I've just told you that it is," snapped Mr. Bascomb.

"Then I say it very respectfully, sir, but pardon me for replying that I don't consider the evidence very convincing. I have shown you why I must have good order in the camp, and I have told you that I do not propose to allow gambling or any other disorderly conduct to go on within camp limits. I can't agree to these things, and then hope to win out by keeping the cost of the work within the appropriation."

"Do you feel that you'll keep within the appropriation by making enemies who deliberately blow up our masonry?" glared Mr. Bascomb.

"I doubt if there will be any more expense in that line, sir. I intend to have such a watch kept over the wall as to prevent any further mischief of the kind."

"Watchmen are an item of expense, aren't they?" snorted the president.

"Yes, sir; but next to nothing at all as compared with the mischief they can prevent."

"I have already told you how to prevent the mischief, Reade. Stop all of your foolish nonsense and let the men have their old-time pastimes."

30

"I can't do it, sir."

"Have you paper, pen and ink here?" thundered Mr. Bascomb. "If so, bring them."

Tom quietly obeyed.

"Reade," again thundered the president of the Melliston Company, "I have had as much of your nonsense as I intend to stand. You are out of here, from this minute. Take that pen and sign your resignation!"

CHAPTER VII

TOM ISN'T AS EASY AS HE LOOKS

"I don't believe I'll do that, sir," murmured Tom, putting down the pen.

"You don't, eh?"

"No, sir."

"Oh, then you'd rather wait and be forced out?"

"How about the contract, sir, between your company and Reade & Hazelton? Contracts can't be broken as lightly as your words imply."

"I'll break that contract, if I set out to," declared Mr. Bascomb, purpling with half-suppressed rage. "I've every ground for breaking the contract. You're running things with a high hand here, and disorganizing all our efforts. No contract will stand on presentation of any such evidence as that before a court."

"I am quite willing to leave that to a court, if I have to," Reade rejoined. His tones were decidedly cold. "Mr. Bascomb, even if I were inclined to forfeit the contract I would have no legal right to do so without the approval of my partner, Hazelton."

"Humph! He's dead," snorted the president.

"That yet remains to be proved, sir," Tom answered huskily, his voice breaking slightly at thought of Harry.

"How on earth do you think you could defend a contract against a wealthy company like ours? Why, we could swamp you under our loose change alone. How much money have you in the world? Two or three thousand dollars, perhaps."

"I've a little more than that," Tom Reade smiled. "For one thing, I'm a third owner in the Ambition mine, on Indian Smoke Range, Nevada, and the Ambition has been a dividend payer almost from the start. Hazelton owns another third of the mine."

"Eh?" gasped Mr. Bascomb, plainly taken aback.

"Oh, we're not millionaires," Tom laughed easily. "Yet I fancy Hazelton and I could raise enough money to fight any breach of contract case in court. With a steady-paying mine, you know, we could even discount to some extent the earnings of future years."

"Oh, well, we don't want hard feelings," urged Mr. Bascomb, his manner becoming more peaceable. "The plain truth is, Reade, that we're utterly dissatisfied with your way of managing things here. When you know how the Melliston Company feels toward you, you don't want to be impudent enough to insist on hanging on, do you?"

"I am certain that I speak for my partner, sir, when I state that we won't drop the contract until we have fulfilled it," Tom muttered, coolly, but with great firmness.

"What's all this dispute about anyway, Bascomb?" a voice called cheerily from the hallway.

"Oh, it's you, is it, Prenter?" asked Mr. Bascomb, turning and not looking overjoyed at the interruption.

Simon F. Prenter was treasurer of the Melliston Company. Tom had met him at the time of signing the engineers' contract with the company. Now Reade sprang up to place a chair for the new arrival.

"What was all the row about?" Mr. Prenter asked affably. He was a man of about forty-five, rather stout, with light blue eyes that looked at one with engaging candor.

"I have been suggesting to Reade that he might resign," replied Mr. Bascomb, stiffly.

"Why?" asked Prenter, opening his eyes wider.

"Because he has raised the mischief on this breakwater job. He has all the men by their ears, and the camp in open mutiny."

"So?" asked Mr. Prenter, looking astonished.

"Exactly, and therefore I have called upon the young man to resign."

"And he refuses?" queried the treasurer. "Most astounding obstinacy on the part of so young a man when dealing with his elder."

"I'll try to explain to you, Mr. Prenter," volunteered Reade, "just what I've been trying to tell Mr. Bascomb."

"I don't know that I need trouble you," replied Mr. Prenter, moving so that he stood more behind the irate president. "I overheard what you were telling him."

Then the treasurer did a most unexpected thing. He winked broadly at the young engineer.

"Yes, Prenter," Mr. Bascomb went on, "this camp is in a state of mutiny. The men are all at odds with their chief."

"Strange," murmured the treasurer of the Melliston Company. "When I paused on the porch, before entering, I thought I caught sight of unusual activity down at the water front. Did you notice it, too, Bascomb?"

"I noticed nothing of the sort," replied the president stiffly. "Am I to infer, Prenter, that you are going to follow your occasional tactics and try to laugh me out of my decision as president of the company?"

"Oh, nothing of the sort, I assure you," hastily protested the treasurer. But he found chance to drive another wink Tom Reade's way. The young chief engineer could not but feel that an ally had suddenly come his way.

"Now, what is the nature and extent of the mutiny?" asked Mr. Prenter.

"First of all, eight thousand dollars' damage has been done to the retaining wall of the breakwater," replied Mr. Bascomb. "That is, according to Mr. Reade's figures, which very likely may prove to be too low. Also, Mr. Hazelton has been murdered."

"Hazelton—-killed?" gasped Mr. Prenter showing genuine concern. "Of course I know that the telegram to the office said that Hazelton was missing, but I didn't suppose it was anything as tragic as a killing."

"Well, Hazelton can't be found, so I haven't a doubt he was killed as part of a general plan of mutiny and revenge on the part of the mixed crews of men working here," declared Mr. Bascomb.

"Oh, I sincerely hope that Hazelton hasn't lost his life here!" cried Mr. Prenter. "Reade, aren't you going to take us down to the water front and show us the extent of the damage?"

"I shall be only too glad to do so, sir," Tom agreed.

Even Mr. Bascomb consented at last to go. As they gained the porch Nicolas rushed up with the cigars for which the president had sent him. While Mr. Bascomb paused to light one, Mr. Prenter thrust an arm through Tom's and led that youth down the road.

"Now, Mr. Reade," murmured the treasurer, earnestly, "Mr. Bascomb, of course, is our president, and I don't want you to treat him with the slightest disrespect. But Bascomb isn't the majority stockholder nor the whole board of directors, so I'll just drop this hint: When Bascomb talks of resignations don't attach too serious importance to it until you receive a resolution endorsing the same view and passed by the board of directors of the company."

"Thank you. I have no intention of resigning," smiled Tom.

"Now, let's go on," continued Mr. Prenter.

Mr. Bascomb, having his cigar lighted, seemed to prefer strolling in the rear by himself.

"Now, I don't want to give you any wrong impressions, Mr. Reade," went on Mr. Prenter. "Mr. Bascomb is the head of our company, but other directors represent more of the stock of the company than he does. I am one of them. Sometimes Mr. Bascomb gets a bit hard-headed, and he is inclined to give orders that others of us wouldn't approve. I judge that you and he were having some dispute when I happened along."

"I didn't regard it as a dispute, sir," Reade rejoined. "In the first place, I had discharged, for incompetency and faithlessness, a foreman named Evarts.

"And Evarts is a pet of Mr. Bascomb's," smiled Mr. Prenter. "I imagine that Evarts is even some sort of family connection who has to be looked after and kept in a good job."

"Anyway," Tom continued, "I explained that Evarts was worse than useless here and that I couldn't have him in the camp or on the job."

"Quite right, I fancy," nodded Mr. Prenter. "In the second place, Mr. Bascomb ordered me to stop my crusade against the gamblers who had tried to invade the camp and rob the men of their earnings. Hazelton and I had that sort of row once out in Arizona—-and we won out."

"You deserve to win out here, too," remarked Mr. Prenter. "I have no patience with anything but straight, uncompromising right. We can't control the men, if they see fit to leave the camp at night, but you have every right—-and it's your duty—-to see to it that no disorder is allowed within camp limits. I, too, have heard something about your trouble here, Mr. Reade, and I can promise you that the directors generally will sustain you. So Mr. Bascomb demanded your resignation?"

"He did, sir."

"Let it go at that," smiled Mr. Prenter. "You may even, sometime, if it will please Mr. Bascomb, hand him your resignation. I will see to it that it doesn't get past the board of directors. Mr. Bascomb is irritable, and sometimes he is a downright crank, but he is valuable to us just the same. We feel, too, Reade, that you and Hazelton are just the men we need to put this breakwater through in the best fashion."

"Even though at least eight thousand dollars in damage was done last night?" queried Tom.

"Yes, even in the face of that. I am certain that you will know how to forestall any more such spite work."

"Now, I'm not altogether so sure of that, sir," Reade answered, quickly. "Of course we'll be eternally vigilant after this, but the trick was done last night so cleverly and mysteriously that we may be surprised again by the plotters. Speaking of mystery, could anything be stranger, or harder to explain, than what happened to poor Hazelton?"

"There *was* mystery for you!" nodded Mr. Prenter. "Have you any ideas whatever on the subject of Hazelton's disappearance?"

"Not the slightest," groaned Tom. "I know all the indications are that he has been killed, and I ought to believe that such is the case. But I simply won't believe it. Why, if he were killed, what became of the body?"

"It's a puzzle," sighed Mr. Prenter.

They were now nearing the land end of the breakwater wall. Mr. Bascomb overtook them. Together the three strolled out along the wall, halting frequently, to observe what the men were doing. It was their plan to keep on until they came to the scene of the two explosions of the night before.

"Just what are you doing here?" asked Mr. Bascomb, stopping and pointing to a gang of men at work on a scow moored against the wall.

"I can tell you, after a fashion, sir," Reade answered. "Yet this was a part of Hazelton's performance. He had charge here, and knew ever so much about it. Poor old Harry!"

Behind them, at the beginning of the wall, a long, loud whistle sounded.

In a moment fully a hundred of the workmen stood up, waved their caps and cheered as though they had gone mad.

Coming forward, with long strides, was Harry Hazelton, in the flesh!

CHAPTER VIII

MR. PRENTER INVESTIGATES

Tom suddenly felt dizzy. He wished to race back, to be the first to greet his chum and press his hand. But just then Reade felt strangely bewildered.

"Of course I don't believe in ghosts!" Tom laughed nervously.

"No!" chuckled Mr. Prenter. "This is real flesh and blood that is coming toward us."

Now, for the first time, Tom Reade knew just how fully he had believed, in the inner temple of his soul, that Harry Hazelton had been actually killed.

"Pulling my work to pieces, are you, Tom?" Harry called jovially.

"P——p——pardon me for not coming to meet you, old fellow, b——b——but I'm dumbfounded at seeing you," Tom called back.

Harry, too, looked rather unsteady in his gait by the time he joined them. The last few yards he tried to run along the wall. Tom thrust out an arm and caught him just in time.

"You've been hurt, Harry!" gasped Tom.

"Yes, and I guess I'm a bit weak, even now," Hazelton mumbled. "Hurt? Look at this."

Hazelton uncovered his head, displaying a court-plaster bandage underneath which clotted blood showed.

"Where in the world have you been?" Tom quivered.

"At sea," Harry answered, with an attempt at banter.

"What happened to you?"

"Tom, you remember the big black man I imagined that I saw last night?"

"Of course I do."

"He was a reality," Harry went on soberly. "After you had gone he appeared again. We had it hot and heavy. I saw your boat coming, and I yelled——"

"I heard you," Tom interposed. "We got along as speedily as we could."

"And you didn't find me," finished Harry. "That brute hit me over the head with something. We clinched and rolled into the gulf together. That was the last that I remember clearly for some time. For a long time I had a dream that I was bobbing about in water, and that I had my arms around a floating log. By and by I came to sufficiently to discover that the dream was a reality. I was holding to the log in grim earnest. How I came to find the log I can't imagine. I think, while more than half unconscious, I must have been swimming straight out into the gulf. Then I must have touched the log and clung to it instinctively. Anyway, when I recovered more fully I knew that the 'long-shore lights looked thousands of miles away. I was too weak even to dream of trying to swim back, or to push the log before me. So I got a stout piece of cord out of one of my pockets and lashed myself to the log. I was afraid I might become unconscious again. A part of the time I was unconscious.

"Well after daylight I saw a sloop headed my way. It didn't look as though it would go straight by either. So I waved my handkerchief——my hat was gone. After a while the skipper of the sloop saw me and headed in for me. It was a sloop that carries the mails to Hetherton, a village that has no rail connection.

"The captain hauled me aboard, questioned me, looked as though he more than half doubted my yarn, and then put me to bed in the cabin of the sloop. He attended to me as best he could. When we reached Hetherton, about noon, a doctor patched me up. I had something to eat, bought this new hat, and hired a driver to take me ten miles to the railway. Then I came over here as soon as I could, and——pardon me, but I'm feeling weak. I'll sit down right here."

Harry sat down heavily on the wall.

"Why didn't you wire me?" asked Tom.

"Why, you didn't doubt but that I'd turn up as surely as any other bad egg, did you?" questioned Harry, looking up.

"Chum, I wouldn't admit it, even to myself, but I feared you were dead. But we mustn't waste time talking. Describe that black man to me, and——"

"And the company will hire detectives to start right on the trail of that negro," interjected Mr. Prenter.

"If——if the expense is really warranted," ended Mr. Bascomb, cautiously.

"Warranted?" retorted the treasurer of the Melliston Company. "Why, it is absolutely necessary to protect our work here! That big negro is the key to the mystery. We must catch him if it costs us a thousand dollars."

"Oh, well," assented President Bascomb, reluctantly.

"I——I guess I'm all right to start in to work now," Harry suggested, trying to rise.

"Sit down——you're not!" replied Tom and Treasurer Prenter, in the same breath, as both pressed Harry back to the wall.

"We don't need work so much to-day," Mr. Prenter continued. "What we want to do is to solve this mystery. You stay here, Hazelton. I'll go back alone and find a 'bus or a carriage. Then we'll go back to camp and hold a council of war. Something must be done, and we'll decide *how* it's to be done."

Mr. Prenter, though no longer a young man, proved that he carried both speed and agility in his feet. While he was gone Tom endeavored to get a few more particulars from Harry, but Hazelton simply didn't know anything that threw any more light on the dread mystery of the breakwater.

"Then a million-dollar undertaking like this is to be constantly imperiled, just because of a senseless moral crusade that you two young men are trying to put through in the camp," declared Mr. Bascomb moodily.

Tom covertly signaled his chum to pay no heed to this remark.

Within a quarter of an hour Treasurer Prenter returned in a stage drawn by two sorry looking horses.

"This will carry us up to the house, if the affair doesn't break down," Mr. Prenter called cheerily. "Come along, folks."

Soon afterwards the four were back on the porch. Nicolas came gliding out to see what he could do for their comfort.

"Just circulate around and make sure that no one gets close enough to hear what we're talking about," Mr. Prenter directed. He had already ordered the driver of the stage to withdraw a few rods and await orders.

"Now, then, Hazelton," continued the treasurer, "we're anxious to hear more of your strange story."

"I've told you all there is to it," protested Harry.

"Surely, there must be some more to it."

"There isn't."

"Then, for the tale of an engineer who was all but murdered, and a case enveloped in mystery from end to end," cried Mr. Prenter, "we have a most singular scarcity of details."

"There are only two more details needed, as it appears to me," Tom remarked quietly.

"Good! And what are they?" demanded the treasurer, wheeling around to look keenly at the young chief engineer.

"The two details we now need," Reade continued, "are, first, who was the negro? Second, who was behind the negro in this rascally work?"

"Only two points to be solved," suggested the treasurer mockingly, "but pretty big points. Of course, the first point is——"

"To find that negro, and get him jailed," Tom declared incisively.

"Good enough!" nodded Mr. Prenter. "The detectives will find the negro."

"Will they?" Tom asked. "Then that will be something new, indeed. I've seen detectives employed a good deal, Mr. Prenter, and generally all they catch are severe colds and items to stick in on the expense account."

"Oh, there are some real detectives in this country," contended Mr. Prenter. "We'll engage some of them, too."

"The expense of hiring detectives will be very large," murmured Mr. Bascomb uneasily.

"Yes, it will," agreed the treasurer with a laugh. "But never mind. It's always my task to find funds for the company, you know."

"Harry," Tom broke in, "just what did that negro look like?"

"About six-foot-three," answered Hazelton, slowly and thoughtfully. "He was broad of shoulder and comparatively slim at the waist. He must weigh from two hundred and twenty-five to thirty pounds. As to age, I couldn't tell you whether he was nearer thirty or forty years. From his agility I should place him in the thirty-year class."

"Any beard?"

"Smooth-faced."

"Scars?"

"I couldn't see that much in the dark."

"Color of his clothes?"

"Some darkish stuff——that's all I can say."

"Could you pick him out of a crowd of negroes?"

"Not if they were all of the same height and weight," Hazelton admitted.

"Do you think you ever saw him before?" Reade pressed.

"I'm sure that I never have," Harry replied.

"Then he wasn't one of our men in this camp at any time?" Mr. Prenter interjected.

"We have never had a man in the camp as large as this negro," Harry rejoined.

"Such a very large black man ought not to be hard for the detectives to locate," Prenter continued.

"Very good, sir. Then you can let the sleuths have a try at the matter," Tom suggested.

"Have you any telegraph blanks here?"

Tom went inside, coming out with a pad of blanks. Mr. Prenter addressed a dispatch to the head of a detective agency in Mobile.

"We'll get the 'bus driver to take this over to town," said Mr. Prenter, as he signed the dispatch.

"You had better send your dispatch by Nicolas, who is so faithful that he can't be pumped, and he never talks about things that he shouldn't."

37

The Mexican was accordingly sent away in the stage. When he returned Nicolas busied himself with getting supper and setting it on the table. Superintendent Renshaw returned from the work in time to join the others at table.

"Mr. Reade, how are you going to protect the works to-night?" inquired the superintendent.

"I'm going to order Foreman Corbett and twenty men to night duty," Tom answered. "The motor boat will also be out to-night. We'll have every bit of the wall watched by men with lanterns."

"What you ought to do," suggested Treasurer Prenter, "is to light the breakwater up with electric lights. You have steam power enough here, and with a dynamo you could supply current to the lights."

"There's the expense to be considered," mildly observed President Bascomb.

"The expense is a good deal less than having the wall damaged by more explosions," said Prenter, rather sharply. "Reade, how long would it take you to get an electric light service going?"

"It ought not to take more than three or four days, sir, if we can pick up a suitable dynamo in Mobile. But there's another point to be considered. We very likely would have to obtain the permission of the Washington authorities before we could run a line of lights out into the Gulf of Mexico. You see, sir, so many uncharted lights might confuse the navigators of passing ships."

"Write Washington, then, and find out where you stand in the matter," directed the treasurer.

"Yes, sir; I'll do that," Reade agreed.

"But don't order any electrical supplies until you've got an estimate of the cost and have it approved by me," hinted President Bascomb. This cautious direction made Mr. Prenter shrug his shoulders.

Dinner finished, all hands went out to sit on the porch. Mr. Bascomb soon began to ask questions about the camp, the housing of the men, and about other details of the camp.

"Although it is dark it's still early. Wouldn't you like to go over through the camp with us?" proposed Tom.

Mr. Bascomb agreeing, the whole party set out, only Nicolas remaining behind to keep an eye over the house.

Though he did not then suspect it Tom was on the threshold of more trouble in the camp.

CHAPTER IX

INVITED TO LEAVE CAMP

Lanterns hung here and there on poles lighted the camp. Men who toil hard all day do not usually want a long evening. Many of the men were already inside their tents or shacks, preparing for bed.

At least two hundred, however, were still stirring in the streets of the camp. Tom led his friends near one of the groups. A warning hiss was heard, and then a man in a remote group, urged by his comrades, rose and staggered toward a shack. Tom was at the man's side in an instant. He proved to be an Italian.

"My man, you appear to be intoxicated," Tom remarked, quietly, as he gripped the Italian by the arm.

"No spikka da English," hiccoughed the laborer. As he spoke he tried to free himself from the engineer's grasp. He staggered, and would have fallen, had not Tom prevented the fall.

"Where's this man's gang-master?" Tom demanded, looking about him sharply, while he still held the drunken man.

None of the Italians addressed appeared to know. For the most part they took refuge in the fact or the pretense that they didn't understand English.

"Get an Italian gang-master, Harry," Tom murmured softly.

Hazelton bolted away, but was soon back, followed by a dark-skinned man who came with apparent reluctance.

"You're a gang-master?" Tom demanded, looking sharply at the man. "This fellow is intoxicated."

"Is he?" asked the gang-master.

"Yes, he is," Tom declared, bluntly. "Now, where did the man get the liquor."

"I do not know," replied the gang-master, shrugging his shoulders.

"Then it's your business to know——if he got his liquor in camp. We won't allow any of that stuff in camp, and you gang-masters all know that."

"I can't stop a man from going to town to get liquor," argued the gang-master.

"No; you can't," Tom admitted. "Neither can I. But it's your duty, gang-master, to see that no liquor is brought back into camp. This man hasn't been to town for the stuff either. He hasn't had time enough to go away over to Blixton and get enough liquor to make him drunk. Moreover, in his present condition, the fellow couldn't have walked back from town the same evening. This man got his liquor in camp, and it will have to be stopped. Now, put this man in his shack; see that he gets into bed. Then come back to me."

The gang-master obeyed.

"We'll see if we can't put a complete stop to this sort of thing," Reade muttered.

"Now, do you think it's going to be well to interfere so much with the movements of the men?" asked President Bascomb, in an undertone. "I am afraid that you'll only start more dissatisfaction and more treachery among them."

"This having liquor in camp is going to be stopped, sir," Tom insisted. "A keg of liquor will demoralize a whole campful of men like these. They are an excitable lot, and they go crazy when there's any liquor around. If we don't put a stop to it, then there'll be fights, and then a few murders are most likely to follow. I've had plenty of experience with men such as we have here, and the stopping of liquor in camp means our only safety, and our only chance to have our work well done. Come along; let the gang-master follow us."

Tom went directly up to a group of workmen who had been looking curiously on. Most of them were Italians, but there were a few negroes present.

"Now; men, gather around me," Tom requested. "I want to talk to you. Come close."

As they did so Reade rested a hand on the shoulder of a negro.

39

"My friend," said Tom, "you've been drinking to-night."

"No, sah, boss! 'Deed I hasn't," replied the negro, earnestly.

"Man, don't you think I have a nose?" Tom demanded, dryly. "Every time you open your mouth I smell the fumes of the stuff. There are other men in this group, too, who have been drinking. I want you all to realize that this sort of thing must stop in this camp. We don't want fights and killings, nor do we want men who wake up so seedy in the morning that they can't do a proper day's work. As I look about me I see at least eight men who have been drinking this evening. That shows me that some one has been bringing liquor into the camp."

Other workmen were now approaching, curious to know what was in the air.

Tom, glancing about him, suddenly, fastened his gaze on one man in particular. This was a lanky, sallow-looking chap of some thirty years.

"See here, just what is your errand in this camp?" Reade demanded, confronting the man.

"Is it any of your particular business?" demanded the fellow, with some insolence in his tone.

"Yes; it is," Reade assured him, promptly. "I'm chief engineer in this camp, and I've asked you what you are doing here!"

"Is it against any law for an outsider to come into camp?" argued the stranger.

"Answer me," Tom insisted, stepping closer. "What are you doing in this camp?"

"I won't tell you," came the surly retort.

"You don't have to," Reade snapped, as he suddenly ran one hand over the sallow man's clothing. Out of the fellow's hip pocket Tom briskly brought a quart-bottle to light. It was about half-filled with some liquid.

"Here, give that back to me!" growled the fellow. "It's mine."

"I'm glad you admit it," rejoined Reade, drawing the cork and taking a sniff as Hazelton slipped in front of him to protect him. "This is liquor. So you're the bootlegger who is bringing this stuff into camp to sell to the men? You won't come here after to-night if I can find any way of keeping you out."

Reade finished his remark by re-corking the bottle and throwing it down hard on the ground. The bottle was smashed to flinders, the liquor running over the ground.

"Here, you! You had no right to do that!" roared the fellow. He made an effort to reach Tom, but Harry gave the fellow a shove that sent him spinning back. "You'll pay me for that stuff, Reade, since you destroyed it."

"How much?" asked Tom, artlessly.

"A dollar and a half," insisted the stranger, coming forward as Reade thrust one hand into trousers pocket.

Tom withdrew the hand, laughing.

"Much obliged, my friend," mocked the young chief engineer. "You've confessed all that I wanted to know. You've tried to charge me the price of a pint of liquor sold in single drinks. That confesses that you've been in camp to sell liquor to the men. I shall pay you nothing, for you're here against the law and against the camp regulations. You're engaged in selling liquor illegally. If I catch you in camp again on that business, my friend, I'll arrest you and hold you until the officers come over from Blixton and take you."

Then, in the next moment, Tom suddenly shot out:

"Harry, see to it that our friend doesn't run away just yet!"

"What are you up to?" demanded the man, as Tom stepped close once more, while Harry rested a hand on his shoulder.

"For a rather warm evening," Reade rejoined, "it strikes me that it's a bit odd for you to be wearing a long top-coat. I'm going to look you over a bit."

"You get out and keep away from me!" blustered the man, raising one of his fists. But Harry caught at that arm and held it. Treasurer Prenter, who had been looking on with keen interest, seized the other arm.

"You let go of me, or you'll run up against the law for assault!" warned the stranger.

His captors, however, held him, while Tom rapidly ran his hands over the stranger's clothing. As a result, within less than a full minute, Tom had removed two full quart bottles and six smaller ones from the fellow's various pockets. All of these the young chief engineer threw on the ground, smashing them.

From the crowd gathered about, which numbered more than sixty men of three different races, a howl went up. President Bascomb began to shiver.

"I'll make you sweat for this!" raved the stranger.

"Let go of the fellow, please," said Tom. Then, as Harry and Mr. Prenter stepped aside, Reade added, "I'll admit, Mr. Bootleg, that I've behaved in a rather high-handed fashion with you. But I'm justified in doing it. You have been breaking the law of the state, moving through this camp and selling liquor. You represent the scum of the otherwise decent population of Alabama. If you think you've any redress in the courts, my name is Reade and you can hire a lawyer and get after me as hard and as fast as you like."

"I'll take personal satisfaction out of you!" stormed the fellow.

"All right," Tom agreed laconically. "You may start now, if you feel like doing it. I'll agree that none of my friends or workmen shall take any part in anything you feel like starting. If you can thrash me then you shall be allowed to depart in peace after you've done it."

Tom did not put up his hands, though he watched keenly to see whether the stranger meant to attack him. The stranger muttered unintelligible threats, then he turned to the laborers pressing about him.

"Men," he demanded, "are you going to be free, or are you going to allow yourselves to be treated like a lot of slaves by this boy?"

"If that's all you've got to say," Tom warned "you may as well start now."

"Start?" scoffed the sallow-faced one. "Where to?"

"Anywhere, outside of this camp," Tom informed him. "You can't stay here any longer, and you can't come here again. If I catch you, again, on this company's property, I'll see to it that you're arrested, and locked up for trespass."

"That's the way to talk!" nodded Treasurer Prenter, approvingly.

"I guess I'll go when I get good and ready," asserted the stranger.

In the front ranks of the crowd pressing around them, Reade now discerned the face of the Italian gang-master with whom he had talked recently.

"What's your name?" Tom demanded, turning about on the gang-master.

"Scipio, sir."

"Then, Scipio, take four men, and escort this fellow out of the camp. Don't use any force unless you have to, but see to it that this fellow leaves camp as quickly as he can walk——or be dragged. Start him now."

Gang-master Scipio plainly didn't like the job, but he liked it better than he did the idea of being discharged. So he spoke to four Italians about him, and the five surrounded the man.

"Hol' on dar, Boss Reade!" spoke up a negro. "Ef yo' carry dis matter too far, den dere's gwine to be a strike on dis wohk. Jess ez dis gemman sez, we ain't no slaves. Yo' try to stop all our pleasures ebenings, an' dar's gwine be a strike——shuah!"

"You may strike right now, if you wish to," Tom retorted, facing the last speaker. "Mr. Renshaw will be prepared to pay you off within hour. Any other man in this camp who isn't content to get along without liquor and gambling may as well strike at the same time. Mr. Renshaw, it's half-past eight. At nine o'clock please be at the house ready to pay off any man who isn't satisfied to live and work in a camp where neither drinking nor gambling is allowed. Scipio, why haven't you started that fellow away from here?"

"Too bigga crowd in front of us," replied the Italian gang-master, shrugging his shoulders.

"Come on, Harry," Tom replied. "We'll see if we can't make a way through the crowd." The two young engineers placed themselves at the head of the squad, and succeeded quickly in opening up a passage through a crowd that seemed to be at least half hostile.

Thus Tom found himself soon face to face with an American.

"Evarts!" Reade cried, angrily. "What are you doing here?"

"I'm here by permission," snarled the discharged foreman.

"Whose permission?" Tom insisted, briskly.

"Mr. Bascomb's," replied Evarts, with a leer so full of satisfaction that Reade didn't doubt the truth of the statement.

"Mr. Bascomb," Tom called, "did you tell Evarts that he might visit this camp?"

"Yes; I did," admitted the president of the company, stiffly.

"Then I'm sorry to say that Evarts has been misinformed," Tom went on. "He *can't* visit this camp. He's too much of a trouble-maker here."

"Shut up your talk!" jeered Evarts roughly. "Don't try to give orders to the president of the company that hires and pays you."

"Mr. Bascomb is the head of the company that employs me," Tom assented. "But I am in charge here, and am responsible, with Mr. Hazelton, for the good order of the camp and the success of the work. Therefore, Evarts, you'll leave camp now, and you won't come back again under pain of being punished for trespass."

"Oh, now see here, Reade——" began Mr. Bascomb angrily, as he started forward. But Treasurer Prenter caught Bascomb by the arm, whispering in his ear.

"Waiting for you, Mr. Bascomb," called Evarts.

"I guess you'd better go," called the president, rather shamefacedly, after his talk with Mr. Prenter. "I guess maybe Reade is right. At all events his contract places him in charge of this camp."

"Humph, Evarts, a lot of good you can do us here, can't you?" sneered the sallow-faced fellow.

Tom looked first at one, and then at the other of the pair.

"So," guessed Reade shrewdly, "Evarts has been at the head of this game of unlawful liquor selling in this camp. There are other vendors here, too, are there?"

"You lie!" yelled the discharged foreman.

"You may prove that, at your convenience," Reade replied, without even a heightening of his color. "For the present, though, you're going to get out of camp and stay out."

"I called you a liar," sneered Evarts, "and you haven't the sand to fight about it."

"Fighting with one of your stripe isn't worth the while," Tom retorted, shortly. "Come along, Evarts. I'll show you the way out of camp."

As Reade spoke he took hold of the ex-foreman's arm gently.

"Leggo of me!" raged the foreman, clenching and raising one of his fists.

"Don't make the mistake of touching me," urged Tom, quietly, "but come along. This way out of camp!"

Evarts swung suddenly, driving a fist straight at Reade's face. But the young chief engineer was always alert at such times. One of his feet moved in between Evarts's feet, and the ex-foreman flopped down on his back.

"Come on, now!" commanded Tom, jerking the fallen foe to his feet. "This time you'll hurry out of camp."

"Are you going to stand for it, men?" yelled Evarts, his face aflame with anger. "Come on—all of you! Show that you're not a pack of cowards and slaves!"

From more than a hundred throats came an ominous yell. The crowd surged around Reade and Hazelton. Mr. Bascomb, seeing his chance, dodged and ran out of the crowd. But Mr. Prenter, with a spring, placed himself at Tom Reade's side.

"Come on, men!" yelled the sallow-faced fellow.

"Run dem w'ite slave-drivers outah camp!" yelled a score of negroes. Yells in Italian and Portuguese also filled the air.

In an instant it was plain that Tom Reade had stirred up more than a hornet's nest.

"Come on, Harry," spoke Tom, firmly. "Let's run this pair out of camp. Then we'll come back and look for more trouble-makers and trouble-hunters! Make way there, men!"

One excitable Italian rushed through the crowd, brandishing a revolver. As alarmed men fell back, the Italian confronted Reade, holding the revolver almost in the latter's face and firing.

CHAPTER X

THE NIGHT IS NOT OVER

Tom winced slightly, as the pistol was discharged, for some of the powder burned his face.

Mr. Prenter, who stood beside him, had knocked up the barrel so that the bullet sped over the heads of the crowd.

In a twinkling Tom had hold of the Italian's arm. He wrenched the pistol away, spraining the Italian's arm. Instantly Tom "broke" the weapon, dropping the cartridges out into his pocket. Then he hurled the weapon as far as he could throw it into the shadows of the night.

"You breaka my arm!" snarled the Italian, showing his white teeth.

"Your face is next!" Tom retorted, letting his fist drive. It caught the Italian on the nose, breaking that member.

"Kill him! Kill Reade!" came the hoarse yell on the night air.

"You'll find it a tough job, men!" Tom called, warningly. "I won't die easily, and I'll take a few men along with me when I go. Now, stand out of the way! I shall consider any man an enemy who blocks my path!"

Tom hit resolutely out, at first. Soon the men crowding about him began to realize that they had taken a large contract on their hands in attempting to cow this young engineer.

Then, too, another element entered into the fight. While there were some wild and troublesome men in camp, there were also many straightforward, excellent fellows among them. There were church-going negroes there, Italians who were thrifty and law-abiding, and Portuguese who loved nothing better than law and order.

The better element among the men came thronging forward, willing and ready to fight under such excellent generalship as they knew they would find with Tom Reade.

Other men, of both stripes, came pouring forth from shanties and tents.

The yells and the shot had alarmed the foremen, who now came along on the run.

"Dill, Johnson!" Tom called, as he saw some of the foremen trying to push or punch their way through the throng. "Help me to run Evarts and this other trouble-hunter out of the camp!"

The menacing yells grew fewer and fainter as the cheers of loyal laborers rose.

The foremen seized both trouble makers and began to run them along with more skill than gentleness.

Tom ran along, keeping his glance on the enraged men of the camp, many of whom followed on the outskirts of the crowd. Harry Hazelton occupied himself in similar fashion.

"Now, you get out of this—-and stay out!" ordered Foreman Dill, giving Evarts a shove that sent him spinning across the boundary line of the company's property.

"You, too!" growled Foreman Johnson, giving the bootlegger a kick that sent him staggering along in his efforts to keep on his feet.

44

It was rough treatment, but Tom's course, all through, had been of the only sort that could break down the threatened riot.

"Now, see if that Italian can be found who fired the shot in my face," Tom called. "I'll know him if I lay eyes on him."

There was a prompt search, but the Italian could not be found.

"If he has left camp, and keeps away, perhaps he'll be safe," Tom announced. "But, if I run across him again I'll seize him, hold him for the officers of the law, and see to it that he's sent to prison for attempted murder."

"Here are two men we want!" called Hazelton.

Tom ran to his chum, who was holding an American by the arm. Mr. Prenter had hold of another.

"Two more of Evarts's bootleggers, eh?" muttered Reade. "Let me see."

On one of the men he found a bottle of liquor. On the other no liquor was discovered.

"Did Evarts pay you fellows a salary, or commission?" Tom demanded.

"Commiss——" began one of the bootleggers, then stopped himself with a vocal jerk. "Evarts? I don't even know who he is."

"Yes, you do," chuckled Tom Reade. "You were on the point, too, of telling us that he paid you a commission on your sales, instead of a weekly wage. Now, my men, I've looked you well over and shall know you again. If I find you in camp, hereafter, you'll be dealt with in a way that you don't like. Savvy? Comprenay? Understand? Now——git!"

"Now, men, get back to your camp," shouted Tom. "To-morrow I'll try to find time for a good and sociable talk with all of you. Try to enjoy your few leisure hours all you can, but remember that the men who can't get along without liquor and gambling are the kind of men we don't want here. Any man who is dissatisfied can get his pay from Mr. Renshaw tonight or to-morrow morning. For those who stood by us I have every feeling of respect and gratitude. Those who thought to fight us——or some of them——will have better sense by tomorrow. We don't want to impose on any man here, but there are some things that we shall have to stop doing. Good night, men!"

Engineers, superintendent and foremen now left the men, going towards their barracks.

"I've a little job for you, Peters, if you don't mind going back into the camp," suggested Tom.

"It's not to go back and fight, single-handed, is it?" Mr. Peters asked, with a smile.

"Nothing like it," Tom laughed. "Peters, we have plenty of really good men among our laborers, haven't we?"

"Scores and scores of 'em, sir——among all three kinds of the men, negroes, Italians and Portuguese."

"I wish you would go back, then, and pick out two of each race——six men in all. They must be honest, staunch and able to hold their tongues."

"Do you want them for fighting, sir?" asked Peters.

"Not a bit of a fight in it. I want them to use their eyes and report to me."

"Going to employ spotters on the camp?" asked Mr. Prenter, quickly.

45

"Not a single spot!" Tom declared with emphasis. "I haven't any use for information turned in by spotters."

"I'm glad to hear you say that, Reade," nodded the treasurer.

"What I want the men for, Peters, is something honest and manly, and with no fighting in it," Tom continued. "I want information, and I'll pay the man well who can bring it to me. Now, go and get your six men. Bring them up to the house within half an hour."

Nodding, Peters turned and strode back.

When the others gained the house where the engineers and superintendent lived the foremen took leave of their chiefs.

As Tom, Harry and Mr. Prenter went up the steps to the porch the front door opened to let out Mr. Bascomb.

"Is that revolting row all over?" demanded the president of the Melliston Company.

"What row?" asked Mr. Prenter, innocently.

"That riot back in camp," shivered Mr. Bascomb. "I simply abhor all fighting."

"So I noticed," commented Mr. Prenter, dryly. "Yes; I believe the trouble is over, unless our young chief engineer intends to stir up something new before bedtime. Do you, Reade?"

"I haven't anything in mind," Tom answered with a smile. "Gentlemen, I am afraid you may think I do things with a high hand. But I have been at this engineering business just long enough to know that I must banish all serious vices from a camp of laborers if I hope to get the best results in work out of the men. So I must tackle some problems rather stiffly, and use my fists when I'm driven to a corner."

"I am not thoroughly satisfied of the wisdom of your course," said Mr. Bascomb slowly.

"Sorry to disagree with you, Bascomb," broke in the treasurer, "but I've had some experience in handling what is called wild labor, and I believe that Reade goes at it in just the right way. I don't believe there are really fifty really wild or troublesome men in that camp. The few bad ones usually start trouble going, and then the good ones are driven into it. Let Reade stop the vices over yonder, in the way that he wants to, and the worst of the crowd will call for their time and leave camp. We shall then have a thoroughly good lot of men left, who'll do more and better work."

"That is," almost whined President Bascomb, "if Reade, in doing what he wants, doesn't stir up so much enmity that we have the rest of our wall blown out into the gulf."

"Mr. Bascomb," put in Tom, "while I must have control of the men and their camp I don't wish to do anything to cast reflection on yourself as the head of the company. May I therefore ask, sir, if there is any especial reason why Evarts should be allowed in this camp?"

President Bascomb fidgeted in the porch chair on which he was sitting.

"I——I don't know of any reason, Mr. Reade, why Evarts should be allowed in camp if his presence prevents you from keeping order as you wish."

"Then you approve, sir, of my intention to keep him out?"

46

"I——I won't question your right to handle the matter as you wish, Mr. Reade," was the president's evasive reply.

"Thank you, sir."

Peters was soon back with the six men——two each of the negroes, Italians and Portuguese. All of them understood English.

Harry described the negro who had attacked him on the retaining wall, after which Tom asked:

"Have any of you men ever seen that negro? Have you any idea who he is, and where he can be found?"

None of the six admitted any knowledge of the mysterious black man.

"Then I want you to keep his description in mind," continued Tom. "Keep your eyes open, at all times, for any chance glimpse of him. The man who brings me information leading to the capture of that big negro will receive a reward of one hundred dollars in gold." "Keep your eyes open, won't you? You may find him prowling around the wall at any time. He may walk out on the wall, or he may be found hiding near in a boat. Watch for him."

All promised eagerly that they would do all in their power to earn the hundred dollars.

"That's what I call good business!" cried Mr. Prenter approvingly, as soon as the foreman and the men had gone.

"Does the hundred dollars come out of the company treasury, Reade, or from your own pocket?" inquired President Bascomb.

"Really I hadn't thought of the matter," answered Tom.

"The company can afford to pay its own bills," broke in Mr. Prenter, rather gruffly.

"It's about time to turn in, isn't it?" asked Mr. Bascomb, striking a match and glancing at his watch.

"I'm going to stay up a little longer, and talk with Reade about the dread mystery of our million dollar breakwater, if he'll let me," hinted Mr. Prenter.

Mr. Bascomb rose as though to go into the house.

"While we're talking about the matter, sir," suggested Tom, "wouldn't it be a good idea for us to stroll down to the beach and look out along the wall to see how Foreman Corbett and his gang are guarding the breakwater to-night?"

"Fine idea," nodded the treasurer of the company.

"Then, if you're all going away, and intend to leave the house alone, I think I may as well go with you," grunted Mr. Bascomb. "I don't exactly like the idea of staying here alone in such troublesome times."

Harry walked beside Mr. Bascomb, while Tom led the way with the treasurer. Mr. Renshaw brought up the rear.

As the party came in sight of the beach and glanced out seaward, they saw many a little, dancing light out on the retaining wall. Each light showed where a workman patrolled under the orders of Foreman Corbett. The latter was aboard the motor boat, "Morton," which ran up and down near the wall, throwing the searchlight over the scene.

"Reade," remarked Mr. Prenter, "I don't see that the enemy have any chance to-night to run in and work harm to our property."

47

Hardly had the treasurer spoken when Tom, looking out seaward, saw a sudden, bright flash of light upward. There was a brief pause——then the sullen boom of an explosion reached their ears.

"Mystery of all mysteries!" choked Tom Reade. "There goes another section of the wall——blown up under our very eyes!"

CHAPTER XI

A MESSAGE FROM A COWARD

"Now Reade," began President Bascomb, in a shaking voice, "what can you say——"

Tom didn't wait to inform him. The young chief engineer was darting out on the wall as fast as he could go.

Already the "Morton" had turned, and was chugging back to the scene of this latest outrage, the searchlight flashing back and forth, in the vain effort to detect any small craft stealing away from the vicinity.

"I——I can't race on a narrow runway like that," faltered Mr. Bascomb, halting at the beginning of the narrow wall. "I——I'll wait here, Mr. Renshaw, will you keep me company?"

"If you so direct, sir," replied the superintendent. "For that matter, what Reade and Hazelton can't find out, out yonder, will probably never be discovered."

"Do you share Mr. Prenter's infatuation for those two young men?" asked the president of the Melliston Company.

"I can't say about that, sir," Renshaw replied, with a puzzled air. "But this much I know——I never worked with two more capable men of any age. They always know what to do, and they never lose their heads."

Mr. Bascomb compressed his lips tightly.

In the meantime Tom, Harry and Treasurer Prenter covered nearly a quarter of a mile along the retaining wall when the motor boat, putting about, picked them up with the searchlight.

Toot! toot! sounded the boat's pneumatic whistle.

"Foreman Corbett is signaling to us to wait and he'll put in for us," said Tom, coming to a halt. Soon the motor craft chugged in alongside, coming close to the wall. Tom, Harry and Mr. Prenter jumped, landing safely aboard.

"How did the enemy come to catch you napping, Corbett?" Tom inquired good-humoredly.

"They didn't catch me napping, sir," protested Foreman Corbett. "It is the strangest thing, sir——that explosion. Why, I had had my light turned on that very part of the wall at least a dozen times in the last half-hour before the blow-out came. Our light didn't pick up a soul around there at any time. What do you suppose I did, Mr. Reade, as soon as the explosion sounded?"

"I saw you turn about and use your search light a lot," Reade answered.

"Did you notice, sir, that I turned the light right up at the sky, first-off?"

"I believe I did notice that," Tom assented.

"It seemed to me, sir, that nothing but an airship could plant a charge of high explosive on the wall in that fashion."

"I don't believe the airship theory will explain it either," said Tom, shaking his head.

"Then what theory can explain it?" asked Mr. Prenter, anxiously.

"I'd pay a reward out of my own pocket for the right answer," Reade replied.

"Then you haven't a theory?" asked the treasurer.

"Not even an imitation of a theory," Tom laughed, shortly.

All this time the motor boat was gliding out toward the scene of the wreck.

"Now, you can see the damage that has been done," suggested Mr. Corbett, turning the light fully on the scene of the latest blow-out. "You see, a long strip of the wall has been cleaned out. Not a trace of the damaged part shows above water."

"It wasn't as big an explosion as the other two, though," Reade declared. "Really, it looks as though the folks behind this found themselves running low on explosives."

"There must be a trace or a clue left," urged Mr. Prenter.

"High explosives don't leave many traces of anything with which they come in contact," muttered Harry. "If we *do* find any traces, I guess it will have to be in broad daylight."

"And I guess that's right," agreed Tom. "Mr. Corbett, did none of your men patrolling on the wall report any signs of strangers?"

"No such report was made, sir."

"At all events, we can be thankful that the explosion didn't blow one or two of our men into the other world," Tom went on.

"Even that is bound to happen if there are many more of these explosions," muttered Corbett, grimly.

"Which is another reason," remarked Tom Reade, "why we're going to solve the mystery of said explosions at the earliest minute that we can."

"One thing is certain," observed Mr. Prenter, with the nearest approach to gloom that he had yet shown. "If you don't soon penetrate this grim mystery, and find a way to stop these outrages, then the wall will be destroyed more rapidly than you can build it."

"The outrages may cease after a while," suggested Harry.

"No," answered Reade. "As long as the unknown enemy feels that he can harass us without much risk of being caught red-handed, just so long will he go on with his outrages—-unless we give in."

"Give in?" asked Mr. Prenter, with a rising inflection in his voice.

"Unless we give in," supplied Tom promptly, "by allowing gambling and rum-selling to go on openly in our camp of workmen."

"Have you any notion of giving in to that extent?" asked Mr. Prenter.

"Not an idea!" retorted Tom Reade promptly. "It wouldn't be my way to surrender to the Devil. I'll fight to the last ditch—-unless your company really prefers to have Hazelton and myself cancel our contract and get out of this work. Do you?"

"*I* don't want you to quit," replied Mr. Prenter positively. "I admire fighting grit, and I want to see you keep hammering away at the work until you win and the job is finished. The board of directors will stand with me on that, if I can sway them. As for Mr. Bascomb, you mustn't take him too seriously. He's a first rate fellow in a lot of ways, but there's no fight in him, and he's a bit close-fisted, too. As for me, Reade, and as far as I can speak for my fellow directors, go ahead, just the way you've started. If you can find any way to hammer camp vice harder than you've been hammering it, then go ahead and do some harder work with your little hammer."

"I'll do it," promised Tom. "Now, Mr. Prenter, I don't believe anything more will happen here to-night——perhaps not for two or three nights. So I think the wisest thing for you to do will be to get back to the house and get some sleep. The same for you, Harry!"

"What are you going to do?" Hazelton wanted to know.

"I?" repeated Reade. "For to-night I'm going to remain up, and be out here around this threatened wall."

"Then that ought to be good enough for me, also," Harry suggested.

"Not much, chum. I'm going to take the night trick for the present, and put on you the burden of all the day work. So you'll need your sleep."

"I can swing the day work easily enough," laughed Hazelton. "It will be all the more easy as the next few days will be taken up simply with repairing the breaks that have been made."

"Swing the boat in toward land, Mr. Corbett," Tom directed the foreman.

At the little landing Hazelton and Mr. Prenter joined the waiting president and superintendent.

"Did you really find out anything?" called Mr. Bascomb eagerly.

"It's as big a mystery as ever."

"There's just one thing we'll have to do," sighed Mr. Bascomb, "and that will be to stop running the camp on a basis of old Puritan laws."

"You talk Reade into it, if you can," chuckled Treasurer Prenter. "You won't find him easy to convince, either."

Tom didn't wait to discuss the matter. Instead, he signaled to Foreman Corbett to run the craft out again.

"If you want to, Corbett," suggested Tom, with a laugh, as the boat moved over the salt waters again, "you might go ashore and go to bed. You can easily claim that you engaged with us as a foreman, and that being captain of a motor boat amounts to breach of contract."

"I'm not fussing," smiled the foreman. "As long as I can sleep daytimes running this motor boat is easier than working."

"It probably will be," nodded Reade, "unless the enemy go in for a new line of tactics."

"Such as what, sir?" asked Corbett.

"If this boat hampers them too much they may decide to send it to the bottom with a torpedo."

"Let 'em try, then," grunted the foreman, giving the steering wheel a turn.

Though Reade remained up until broad daylight no further sign of the unknown enemies was seen. Through the night, had it not been for the patrols walking up and down the line of wall with lanterns, it would have been hard to realize that the big breakwater was haunted by any such desperately practical group of "ghosts."

"I guess we've heard the last of the rascals," suggested Harry Hazelton one night at supper. Messrs. Bascomb and Prenter had returned to Mobile, so that the young engineers and their superintendent were the only men at table.

"My guess is about the same," drawled Mr. Renshaw.

"Yes?" queried Reade. "Guess again!"

"Oh, I believe they've quit," argued Mr. Renshaw. "For one thing, the scoundrels probably have discovered that detectives from Mobile are down here trying to run 'em to earth. That has scared the rascals away."

"What are the detectives doing, anyway?" asked Harry.

"Blessed if I know," Tom yawned. "I believe there are three of them here or over in Blixton, but I wouldn't know one of them, if I fell over him. The detectives came, secured their orders from Mr. Prenter, and went to work——or pretended to go to work. I'm glad that I'm not responsible for the detectives."

Nicolas entered, an envelope in his hand.

"Par-rdon, Senor Reade," begged the Mexican. "I would not interrupt, but on the porch I found thees letter. It is address to you."

Tom took the envelope and scanned it, saying:

"The address is printed——probably because the writer didn't want to run the risk of having his writing identified. Probably the letter, also, is printed. Pardon me, gentlemen, while I open this communication . . . Yes; the letter is printed, and unsigned——a further sign of cowardice on the part of the writer. And now let me see what it says."

Tom spent a few moments in going through the communication. A white line formed around his mouth as he read. Then he passed the letter to Harry, who read it aloud, as follows:

"You have had a week of peace. Is peace better than war? You may have all the peace you wish, and go on working and prospering if you will let others do the same. Stop interfering with the right of your men to amuse themselves and all will be well. Try any of your former tricks in the camp, and then you will have good cause to 'Beware!'"

"Is that a declaration of war?" asked Harry, looking up.

"I think so," nodded Tom.

"Then how are you going to meet it?"

"There's only one way," Tom returned. "A declaration of war must be met with a fight. Unless I'm very greatly in error the gamblers and bootleggers will try to start up matters again to-night in camp."

"And you'll throw them down harder than before?" queried Mr. Renshaw, gazing keenly at the young chief.

"If it be possible," Tom declared. "Nicolas, be kind enough to go over and ask the foremen to report here at 8:20 promptly. At 8:30 we will enter camp and see what is going on."

"I miss my guess, then," chuckled Mr. Renshaw, quietly, "if our arrival isn't followed by war in earnest."

"War is never so bad," retorted Tom Reade, his jaws setting, "as a disgraceful peace!"

51

CHAPTER XII
AN ENGINEER'S FIGHTING BLOOD

Just at half-past eight that evening Tom, Harry, the superintendent and the foremen entered camp.

They went, first, to a shack which they knew to be occupied by orderly, respectable blacks.

"Come, men," said Tom, halting in the doorway. "I've an idea we may need you."

Six negroes rose and came forward.

"There are gambling and bootlegging going on in this camp to-night, aren't there?" Reade inquired.

"Ah doan' rightly know, boss," replied one of the negroes cautiously.

"But you suspect it, don't you?" Tom pressed.

"Yes; Ah done 'spec so, boss," grinned the negro.

"And I do, too," rejoined Tom. "Come along. We may need a little help."

With this reinforcement—-the negroes were wanted for work rather than for fighting—-Tom now stepped off briskly through the camp.

Nor did he have to guess in which way to go through the darkened streets of this little village of toilers. Shouts of laughter and the click of ivory dice and celluloid chips signaled the direction.

The largest shack in the village was closed tightly as to door and window, though light came out through the chinks. Tom stepped over there boldly, not turning to see whether his following were close behind him.

Stepping up to the closed door the young chief engineer placed his shoulder against it. He gave a sturdy push, and the barrier flew open.

There were about fifty of his men crowded into one large room. A half dozen gambling games were in full blast. At two tables stood bootleggers, each with a bottle of liquor and glasses.

Tom stalked boldly in, still without turning to look at his own following. Reade's face bore such a mild look that the leader of the visiting gamblers was wholly deceived as he glanced up.

"The chief!" called one workman, in dismay, and a dozen men made a break for the door. But Harry and the others prevented their getting out.

"Oh, it's all right," cheerily announced the leader of the gamblers. "Mr. Reade has just come here to look on and make sure that everything is being conducted above board and on the square. Isn't that so, Reade?"

"Yes," Tom assented, pausing near the central table at which gambling was going on.

At that assurance the panic-stricken gamblers breathed more easily. Several men who had jumped up from their seats went back to their chairs.

"Reade is a good friend of ours," called the leader of the gamblers, mockingly. "He isn't going to interfere with any amusements that are properly carried on—- eh, Reade?"

The fellow stared boldly into Tom's eyes, a look of insolent mockery on his features.

"Certainly I'm not going to interfere with any proper amusements in this camp," Tom nodded, easily.

"What did I tell you, boys?" laughed the leader of the gamblers. "Go on with your play, boys!"

"But gambling isn't a proper amusement for poor men, who have to toil and sweat for every five-cent piece they get," Tom Reade continued calmly. "Neither is the trade of bootlegging a decent one, or one that provides decent amusement. I have already warned you that gambling and liquor selling are things of the past in this camp."

There was another stir in the room. The leader of the gamblers rose, fixing his gaze on Tom's eyes and trying to stare the young engineer out of countenance.

"What do you mean, Reade?" he demanded.

"Isn't my meaning clear enough?" Tom insisted, with a chilly smile.

"Man, haven't you come to your senses yet?" snarled the gambler.

"Do you mean to ask whether I was scared by the cowardly, unsigned letter that I received this evening?" Tom fired back at the fellow, with another taunting smile.

"I don't know anything about any letter," muttered the gambler sullenly, "but I heard that you had come to your senses."

"Whether I have or not," retorted Tom, "you are pretty sure to come to your proper senses to-night. Men—-I mean workmen, not gamblers or bootleggers—- you are at liberty to pass out of this building."

"Don't you go," shouted the gambler, as some two dozen men started toward the doorway where Harry and the rest were on guard.

Some of them halted.

"I must have made a mistake in calling some of you 'men,' since you take orders from such disreputable characters as these gamblers and bootleggers," Tom taunted them mildly. "Now, all I will say is that those of you who wish to do so may pass outside. The rest may remain here, though they'll be sorry, afterwards, that they stayed. All who want to get outside must do so at once."

"Don't you do anything of the sort," shouted the gamblers' leader. "Stay here like men and assert your rights! Come on! I'll lead you, and show you how to throw these meddlers out."

"You'll do it—-just like this, eh?" demanded Tom Reade.

He made a leap for the leader of the gamblers, catching the fellow by the throat and waist. Lifting him, Tom hurled the fellow a dozen feet. The gambler fell on one side, but was up in a moment, his right hand traveling toward a hip pocket.

"Don't draw," mocked Tom, with another smile. "Probably you haven't a pistol there. If you have, you can never make me believe that you have sand enough to draw and shoot before as many witnesses as I have on hand."

"I've a good mind to drill you with lead!" scowled the gambler, still resting his hand behind him.

"But you're a wise man," mocked Reade, "and wise men often change their minds."

53

However, the very move of the gambler to draw a pistol had had one effect that Tom ardently desired. Most of the workmen present were now in frantic haste to get out before any shooting began. The two bootleggers also sought to make their escape.

"Get back there! You fellows can't get out!" Harry shouted, himself seizing and hurling the bootleggers back into the room. They rose, glaring sullenly at Hazelton. But they didn't know how many more men he might have behind him out there in the dark.

Tom Reade now had the six gamblers and the two bootleggers in the room with him.

"You're a nice crew, aren't you?" he jeered, gazing at them scornfully.

"We're making our living," retorted the leader of the gamblers, with what he meant to be a fine tone of scorn.

"Making your living off of human beings! You're some of the parasites that infest honest workingmen. I've drummed you out of this camp before, and you have the cheek to come back. Now, I'll try to teach you another lesson. Harry, send in our workmen, will you?"

Hazelton stepped aside, to let in the half dozen honest negroes they had brought along with them. These men entered, then stood looking at their young chief.

"Get hold of those cards, chips and dice!" ordered Tom.

"Here, what are you trying to do?" demanded the leader of the gamblers.

"You have the advantage of me," responded Tom. "I don't know your name."

"Hawkins is my name," replied the chief of the gamblers.

"Hawkins is a fine name," admitted Tom. "It will do as well as any other. I won't annoy you, Hawkins, by asking you what your name used to be in prouder and happier days."

"What are these men doing with our outfit?" insisted Hawkins, as the negroes began industriously to clear the surfaces of the tables.

"You can see what they're doing," Tom rejoined.

"You blacks get out and leave our property alone," warned Hawkins, darting among them.

The negroes drew back, in some alarm, for the gambler looked dangerous with one hand at his hip pocket.

"Go get on with your work, men," counseled Tom. "I'm here to back you up."

"As for you, sir——" snarled Hawkins, facing Tom.

"Don't look at me like that," laughed Reade softly. "Save that face to frighten children with."

The negroes had busied themselves until they had gathered up all the implements of gambling and had stuffed them into their pockets.

Now Tom went up to the bootleggers. Both men he boldly searched, bringing forth from their pockets bottles of liquor. These he threw down hard on the floor of the cabin, smashing them.

"I don't know why we allow you to do all this, Reade," fumed Hawkins, whose face was white with rage.

"It's because you're afraid, and know that you can't help yourselves," Tom smiled.

"I'll show you who's afraid!" yelled Hawkins, again throwing his right hand back to his hip pocket.

This time Reade saw the unmistakable butt of a revolver. Without an instant's hesitation. Reade leaped at the fellow. In a moment Tom had the revolver, springing backwards.

"Well—-shoot!" jeered Hawkins. "You don't dare to."

"You're right," assented Tom coolly. "I don't dare to. Assassination belongs to the lowest orders of human beings. An honest man seldom has any need of concealed deadly weapons."

Tom stepped still farther back, breaking the revolver and dropping the cartridges into one hand. Hawkins made a move as though to spring upon him, but Harry leaped into the room, confronting the gambler.

Thus shielded, Tom drew a combination tool-knife from one of his pockets, then coolly drew out the screw that held the trigger in place.

Dropping the trigger into his own pocket, Tom tossed the weapon back.

"Catch it, Hawkins," he called. "You may want this to frighten some children with over in Blixton. Now, Mr. Renshaw, I believe you know what you're to do."

"Yes, sir," nodded the superintendent, from the doorway, and vanished.

"We'll take our leave, now," sneered Hawkins, "unless you have some further humiliation in store for us."

"Just one," Tom declared, "so you can't go just yet."

"Oh, all right," Hawkins laughed fiercely. "You'll have to pay for this unlawful detention."

"You can tell the officers all about that," Tom suggested tantalizingly. "Mr. Renshaw has just gone to telephone for them."

"The officers? Police?" snarled Hawkins.

"Yes. Did you imagine that you could keep on defying all the laws? You've just threatened me with a taste of the law. You may try a taste yourself, Professor Hawkins!"

"Let us out of this place!" insisted Hawkins angrily. "Come on, friends!"

He rallied his own force of seven men and started toward the door.

"Of course you can try to get away," Reade warned the fellow. "But the effort will cost you all broken heads, to say the least. I have placed you all under arrest for breaking the laws of Alabama, and, before we'll let you go, we'll break a few bones for each of you."

Outside the workmen of the camp were thronging by this time. Doubtless, had they dared, two or three score of these men would have fought in behalf of the gamblers and bootleggers, but far more than that number would have rallied under Tom Reade's banner, for it is human nature to flock to the banner of the leader who is resolute and unafraid. Besides, there were the foremen, all of them good, hard hitting men.

"Oh, well," sneered Hawkins, "let it go at that, Reade. We'll have our day in court tomorrow, and then. I guess we'll find our innings."

"Yes," chuckled Tom, "and when you get your innings you'll be wild to swap them for outings——for the innings will be in jail."

"Don't push my temper too far," cautioned Hawkins with a scowl.

"Let it go as far as you like, always being ready to take the consequences," Tom smiled genially.

There followed a period of tense waiting. After nearly a half an hour of this a 'bus arrived, with four police officers from Blixton in it. Tom Reade preferred his charges against the gamblers and bootleggers. The officers had no choice but to take them, so the late troublemakers, now amid jeers and hoots from many of the workmen, were led outside and into the 'bus.

"You'll hear from this!" hissed Hawkins, in the young chief engineer's ear.

"I believe you," nodded Tom thoughtfully.

After the police and their prisoners had gone Tom led his own party back to the house.

"You'd better get to bed now, Harry," Reade advised his chum. "There can be no telling how soon I'll need to call you up, and you ought to have some sleep first."

"You look for trouble to break to-night?" Harry asked.

"Between now and daylight," said Tom simply.

"Whee! I'd like to stay up with you."

"You might find more fun that way, Harry, but the work to-morrow would suffer, and work is more important than mere fun," Tom answered.

Nor was Tom to be disappointed in his expectation that the worst trouble yet experienced would break loose that night.

CHAPTER XIII

WISHING IT ON MR. SAMBO

"Oho!" breathed young Reade, as he crouched low behind the fringe of bushes, peering toward the beach.

It was now somewhat past midnight. For three hours Tom had been scouting stealthily along this shore section, well to the west of the breakwater.

For, in pondering over the explosions, Tom had come to the conclusion that the blow-outs on the retaining wall, however accomplished, were controlled from a point to the westward of the sea wall.

This conclusion had been rather a simple matter to a trained engineer. Tom had witnessed the flash of one explosion, and that, as he remembered, had sprung up at the west side of the wall. Moreover, the appearance and condition of the wall, at the point of each explosion, had shown that the attack in each case must have been made at the west side of the wall.

And now, after nearly three hours of work, Tom Reade had come upon a real clue.

"Another blow-out is arranged for to-night, just as I had expected," Reade muttered, with an angry thrill, as he glanced at a figure down on the beach. "Moreover, my guess that the huge negro is the fellow who touches off the blow-outs has proved to be the correct one."

Down on the beach a big, black man was moving about stealthily. Though the spot was a lonely one, this scoundrel plainly intended to take no unnecessary risks of detection.

Just at the present moment the negro was placing in the water a curious-looking little raft that he had brought on one shoulder from its place of concealment. It was something like a flat-bottomed scow, the sides being just high enough to prevent whatever cargo it carried, from rolling off into the water.

The raft placed and secured to the shore, the negro crouched in his hiding place in a jungle of bushes. He soon reappeared, carrying four metal tubes.

"The explosive is in the tubes," guessed Tom easily. "And at one end of each tube is a sharp metal point that permits of being driven into the crevices in the wall. Four, or more, of these tubes are thrust into the wall, I suppose, and connected in series, so that they can be fired by the same electric spark. These tubes and the wires are water-proofed. The negro is only the dastardly workman in this case. It was never he who invented the trick. But he must be an excellent workman, who ought to be employed in much more honest effort. I wonder if the fellow is going to use more than four tubes?"

All of these thoughts ran through the mind of Tom as he crouched, peering eagerly at the negro.

By this time the negro was taking to the water, towing his miniature scow and its explosive cargo as he swam.

"He must be a good swimmer, and also a good diver," concluded Tom. "With my men patrolling the sea wall he must have to dive, some distance away, swim under water, and remain there until he has secured one of the tubes in place. Then he has to get back, out of range of the lanterns' rays, and get his breath before he goes back to the next job. But maybe I can interfere with his work to-night."

Though he rose and moved away, Reade, despite the darkness of the night, was careful to keep himself concealed behind the bushes, so that he could not be observed from beach or water. Shortly the young engineer was over at the point in the jungle from which he had seen the negro emerge with scow and explosives.

"The fellow must use a magneto, attached to wires running under the water," concluded Tom. "At that rate, the first real job is to find the magneto. My, but Mr. Sambo Ebony may be wondering, to-night, why his blow-out doesn't work as easily as usual!"

Simple as the search ought to have been, Tom Reade was soon on the point of despair.

"If it isn't a magneto, or if I can't find it in time," Tom muttered uneasily, "the mystery may remain nearly as great as ever, and the explosion may be pulled off to-night, after all."

Twenty minutes passed before Reade, with all his senses alert, stumbled on the concealed magneto. It had been so well hidden, under a mass of rocks, that it would not have been astonishing had Tom missed it altogether.

57

Attached to the magneto was the wire that must connect, in some way, with the series of tubes that would soon be fastened in the retaining wall out yonder. Yet this wire ran into the ground, and then vanished.

"Now, I've simply got to hustle!" sighed Tom Reade nervously. "If I don't succeed in raising the wire, and in a mighty short space of time, I may be tonight's fool yet. I'd really like to wish that on the black man, too!"

By using his eyes and his reasoning powers Reade, after twenty minutes more of search, with some sly digging, unearthed a section of the wire some dozen feet from the magneto.

"Now, it must be really the swiftest sort of work," murmured the young engineer, after a glance seaward. He seated himself with his face turned toward the Gulf, gathered the exposed section of wire up into his lap, then drew a pair of wire nippers from his pocket.

Snip! Tom now had two ends of wire in his hands. That would have been enough, had Reade chosen to bury the ends and conceal all evidence of his work. However, he believed that a more workmanlike way could be found.

From the same pocket Tom drew out a three inch piece of pure rubber cable, wrapped in water-proof tape. This he fastened to the severed ends of the wire, binding the whole as neatly as a lineman could have done.

"Rubber is believed to be a pretty good insulator," chuckled Reade, as he finished. "I don't believe the spark is made that can jump three inches of rubber. Certainly magneto-power can't do it. Now, let me see what sort of a trail-concealer I am."

Tom laid the wire back in the ground, covering it carefully with his hands.

"I wish I dared strike a match, so that I could judge better just how my work looks," he sighed. "However, I don't believe Mr. Sambo Ebony will think it discreet to strike any matches either, so he won't find the place where I've been fooling with his work.

"Now, I'll get back out of sight, where I belong," muttered Tom, rising cautiously. "I hope, though, I can find a place where I can see the look on that darkey's face when he tries his magneto and waits for the bing! from out yonder. Oh, Sambo, you simply can't have any idea of how I've been wishing it on you tonight!"

As the bushes grew thickly hereabouts, and there were many hollows in the surface of the earth, Reade had little trouble in finding what he believed to be a satisfactory hiding place. It enabled him to hide his head within fifteen feet of the handle of the magneto.

A soft, southerly wind blew in from the Gulf. As long as he could Reade fought drowsiness. Again and again he opened his eyes with a start.

"I mustn't do this," Tom told himself angrily. "No gentleman will go to sleep at the switch——when it's his train that is coming!"

Yet still he found himself nodding. Had he deemed it safe Tom would have sprung up and walked about briskly. But this, he knew, was to invite being discovered by the returning negro.

So, at last, despite himself, Tom fell asleep.

58

How much time had passed he never knew. At last, however, he awoke with a start. Reproachfully he rubbed his eyes.

"Not a bit too soon!" he muttered, as his ears caught sound of an approaching step, and his eyes showed him the hulking form of the massive foe. "Here comes my black man!"

CHAPTER XIV

THE BLACK MAN'S TURN

Closer to the earth Tom tried to burrow. As to a plan, Tom Reade had none now, save to watch, and, if possible, to learn something that he did not already know.

Soft-footed, despite his great bulk, the negro approached with an air of little concern. Plainly, the wretch did not much fear discovery——still less interference.

Humming an old plantation melody the negro reached his concealed magneto, then stood up for a brief moment, staring seaward in the direction from which he had just come. His garments dripped water; his whole appearance was bedraggled, yet there was something utterly shaggy, majestic, in this huge specimen of the human race.

"Ah done reckon dem gemmen gwine lose some mo' of deir wall to-night," chuckled the negro softly.

"Go as far as you like, Mr. Sambo Ebony!" grinned Tom Reade, under his breath. "I've wished something else on you this time."

Carelessly the negro bent over his magneto, seized the handle and gave a push.

Then he straightened up, listening. Only the soft sighing of the southern wind came to his ears.

"Yo' shuah done gotta use a mo' greasy elbow dan dat, chile," chuckled this imp of Satan aloud, though in a soft voice that seemed out of all proportion to his bulk.

Then he gave a half dozen indolent though steady strokes to the handle of the magneto.

"Whah am dat 'splosion?" he asked himself in wonderment. "Am mah eardrum done gone busted? Moke, yo' am plumb lazy this night!"

This time the huge negro pumped at the handle of the magneto until he was all but out of breath. Several dozen shoves he had administered before he halted, let go of the magneto and raised himself to his full, majestic height.

"Some black witch hab done gwine wish a big hoodoo on me!" grunted the negro suspiciously. "Dis am do fust time dat de magernetto gwine back on me like dis!"

In his bewilderment the one whom Tom had named Sambo glared around him. His eyes gleamed with a phosphorescence like that which one sees on the water on a lowering night. What Reade did not know was that this black man possessed eyes that were a little keener in the dark than a bat's.

With a sudden "Woof!" Sambo went up in the air, moved sideways, and came down on the startled Tom Reade with the force of a pile driver.

"Wha' yo' doing heah?" demanded the negro, gripping Reade by the coat collar and dragging that hapless engineer to his feet.

Tom did not answer. To save his life he couldn't have answered just then, his breath utterly gone.

"Wha' yo' want heah, anyway?" insisted Sambo, giving the youth a vicious shake.

There was blood before the negro's eyes, or he would sooner have recognized his victim. But at last he did see.

"So, I'se gwine cotch Mistah Reade himself!" snorted Sambo. "An' Ah reckon I'se gwine foun' de differculty wid my magernetto at de same time! Huh?"

Again he shook Tom, with an ease and yet a force that further drove the breath from the young engineer's body.

"Why doan' yo' talk!" glared the negro, holding Tom out at arm's length with one hand.

Tom could only groan. Yet that method of communication carried its own explanation to the big black.

"Reckon yo' gwine talk w'en yo' get gale enough in yo' lungs," grinned the negro. "In dat case Ah gwine lay yo' down on de groun' to fin' yo' breff."

Sambo's idea of laying Tom down was to give him a violent twist that brought the lad flat on the ground at his captor's feet. Then the negro sat on his captive to make sure that the latter did not escape.

"Take yo' time——ah got plenty," grimaced the black man.

Slowly the beaten-out breath came back to Tom Reade. Sambo, watching, knew finally that his quarry was at last able to talk.

"Wha' yo' do to mah magernetto?" demanded Sambo.

"Guess," breathed Tom.

"Oh, take yo' time, boss. Ah got plenty ob dat accommerdation"

"What magneto are you talking about?" Reade queried innocently.

"Nebber heard ob it befo', eh, boss?"

"I've heard of plenty of magnetos, of course," admitted Tom. "But what have you to do with one?"

For a brief instant Sambo was almost inclined to believe that Reade did not fully know his secret. Finally it dawned on the brain of the big black man that he was being hoaxed.

"Ef yo' doan wanter tell, yo' doan hab to, ob co'se," proposed Sambo. "It ain't mah way to be too persistency wid de w'ite quality gemmen. But Ah done thought maybe yo' know somethin' dat yo's burnin' to tell."

"Who are you, and what are you doing around here?" asked Tom. "I'm certain you don't belong to my force of workmen——unless you just joined yesterday. Are you working on the breakwater job?"

"Yessah," promptly answered Sambo with momentary gravity. Then his mood changed to a chuckle.

"Dat am all right, Massa Reade," he allowed. "But yo' doan' fool dis nigger as easy as yo' maybe think. Ah know what yo' watchin' me fo', and Ah done know I'se been doin' jess w'at yo' think. So I guess we doan' need no mo' conversationin', unless yo' willing to talk right out and tell me w'at's w'at."

"Sambo," said Reade solemnly, "I imagine I'm not very intelligent, after all. I listened to you attentively, but, for the life of me, I couldn't make out what you were talking about."

"Kain't yo'?" the negro demanded, mockingly. "Den Ah done reckon Ah must be a good deal of a scholar, ef Ah can talk so dat er w'ite quality gemmen kain't undahstan' me."

Mr. Sambo Ebony chuckled gleefully in appreciation of his own joke.

"There's one thing I guess you can tell me, Sambo," Reade suggested hopefully.

"W'at am dat, massa?"

"When are you going to change your seat and stop making me feel like a very thin pancake?"

"W'en Ah done get mah mind made up."

"When you have your mind made up about—-what?"

"About w'at I'se gwine do wid yo', Massa Reade."

"Well, what do you think you're going to do with me?" insisted Tom. "I'll admit, Sambo, that I'm about losing my patience. Unless you get up off of me soon, and move away to a respectful distance, I shall be obliged to do something on my own account."

"Go as far as yo' like, massa," returned the negro, unmoved. "I'se boun' ter admit dat yo' done got me fo' curiosity. W'at yo' done think yo' *can* do?"

Plainly the negro meant to go on having sport with him. Tom decided that it would be of no use to try to deceive this great mountain of black flesh. So Reade, who had been doing some brisk thinking during the last few moments, gave a sudden heave—-a trick that he retained from the old football days.

Much to Sambo's surprise he found himself going. Yet the black man was as agile as he was big. He leaped to his feet, bounding one step sideways, while Tom, who had been watching for this very chance, sprang to his own feet.

"Not so fas', massa!" mocked the big black, reaching out and taking a strong clutch on. Tom's coat collar.

Reade would have squirmed out of his coat and placed more distance between them, but Mr. Ebony, with a stout twist, gathered the two ends of the coat collar, holding the young engineer as though in the noose of a halter.

Quick as a flash Reade struck out with his right fist for the black man's belt-line. Had the blow landed even the huge Sambo would have gone down to earth. But the negro parried with his own disengaged fist, then gave a twist to the coat collar noose that made Reade turn black in the face from choking.

"Ah might as well tell yo'," Sambo observed dryly, "dat yo' ain't done got no new fight tricks dat yo' can wish on me. Ah done seen all de tricks of fightin' dat any man done know, an' Ah nebber yet seen no man dat could put any kind oh a blow ober on me to hurt!"

The negro spoke boastfully, yet there could be no doubt that he believed all he said.

Tom Reade next schemed to land a hard kick against the negro's shins. Ere he had his foot well lifted, however, the watchful Sambo seemed to divine the intent. He gave a quick twist at the coat collar that made Reade's head swim. It was some time before the young engineer's head recovered from that sudden confusion and blackness.

"Am' yo' gwine beliebe dat yo' kain't wish no kind oh a trick ober on me?" demanded the black man in an injured tone. "Ah nebber seen no odder w'ite man dat had such a ha'd time beliebing w'at Ah done tole him!"

"I've got to land this wicked brute, some way, or I may as well conclude that the jig is danced through, as far as I am concerned," Reade thought ruefully.

Panting, quivering, in dread of being choked again, and much harder, Tom tried to think fast in the effort to devise some new plan for worsting this terrible opponent.

"I've been fooling myself all along," Tom told himself, with a sinking heart. "I've been up against several men who were too weak or too cowardly to fight, and I've somehow gained the opinion that I could fight. But this black fellow has taken all the conceit out of me. I was a fool ever to think that I could fight! I'm nothing but a piece of jelly——or putty!"

Of a sudden Reade tried to wrench himself free at the collar, at the same time raising his right knee with a forceful jerk. He wanted to drive that knee into the black man's wind.

But Sambo seemed to guess the plan without trouble. He gave a twist that choked Tom, once more, until all went black before him. Then the negro slammed his victim down hard on the ground, well-nigh stunning the young engineer.

"Ah done see w'at Ah gotta do wid yo'," Sambo announced. "Ah gotta tie yo' up, load yo' pockets wid rocks, and den take yo' out in de Gulf ah' lose yo'! Dat's w'at Ah gotta do, an' Ah ain' gwine lose no time about it either."

Sambo was in earnest, too. He had mapped out that very course!

CHAPTER XV

A DAVID FOR A GOLIATH

From his pockets the big fellow brought out a coil of stout cord. Without much trouble he slipped a noose over one of Tom's wrists. Then began an active fight, the object of which, on the black man's part, was to make the other wrist secure.

But here Tom developed an amount of agility and a skill in fighting that angered Sambo.

"Doggone yo', ef yo' won't take it peaceable-like, den yo'll get it do odder way."

With that, Sambo delivered a blow that made young Reade see stars. His head swam dizzily. Now, the black man secured the other wrist, making a turn and a knot that would have done credit to an expert.

But about that time something else happened. Whack! A blow from a club landed across the negro's head.

"Who doin' dat?" demanded the negro, blinking and half turning.

"I did eet, you miser-r-r-rable black smoke, and I do eet again!" rang the voice of Nicolas, as that valiant Mexican circled around the negro.

"Yo' blow away, yaller baby!" jeered Sambo, whose head had been not at all hurt by the blow.

"I show you eel I run away!" bridled up Nicolas.

Tom now began to recover enough to know that his faithful servant was on the scene.

"Scoot, Nicolas!" urged Tom, in a gasping Voice. "Run for all you're worth. This fellow will eat you up. Run and bring help."

"Senor, I can wheep him with one hand!" vaunted the little Mexican.

"Run, I tell you, and get help. Be like a flash, man!"

"As you say, Senor, but——"

Nicolas turned, speeding away.

His escape, however, would interfere, possibly, with the plans of Sambo. The big black leaped up, racing after Nicolas.

As the Mexican was a little fellow, and short of leg, it was not long before the pursuer caught up with him.

"Hol' on, yo' yaller rascal!" laughed Sambo, reaching out for the Mexican.

Nicolas wheeled about, dancing out of reach of the negro's massive hands.

"Stand still, yo' li'l' Greaser!" laughed Sambo.

"Now you have insult me, and I show you what I do to you!" snarled Nicolas, his brown face aflame at the taunting word, "Greaser."

"Come heah!" jeered Sambo, making a bound and reaching for the small man.

Nicolas dodged, but he did not run away. Instead, he bobbed up inside of the negro's reach. The Mexican thrust out his slim, sinewy right-hand forefinger. A vicious poke he gave with it, landing sharply on a spot just about an inch and a quarter below the base of the negro's breast bone.

"Woof!" panted Sambo, half doubling, for Nicolas had touched a tender spot.

"You have insult me! You call me mean name!" raged Nicolas. "Stand steel, you big black smoke!"

Again Nicolas ducked and rushed in. Once more he employed his forefinger tip in the same fashion, and with more power.

"O-o-o-o-o-h! Wow!" gasped Sambo, this time doubling nearly to the ground. "Get away, chile! I doan' wan' no mo' ob yo'!"

"You have insult," insisted Nicolas angrily, "and I do much more yet to you."

This time the negro appeared almost helpless. Nicolas danced about, looking for an opening. In desperation Sambo struck out with his powerful left. It gave the Mexican the chance he wanted. Darting in, he repeated his trick for the third time.

The bulky negro lay down, groaning. He had too little breath left to be dangerous.

While this was going on Tom Reade had rolled over on his face. From this position he succeeded in getting to his knees. Then he rose and hastened toward the Mexican.

"Nicolas, you're surely a little terror!" Reade admitted, admiringly. "Now, untie my hands and we'll take care of Sambo."

"Wait——jus' one leetle moment, Senor," begged the Mexican. He turned back to Sambo, that forefinger ready for another jab.

"Fo' de lub ob goodness——" gasped Sambo. But Nicolas was determined. He made the jab, and Sambo all but lost the little breath that was in him.

"Now, Senor, we do it all in one second," proclaimed the Mexican. From his pocket he drew a knife, springing the blade open. Snip! snip! and the young engineer was free of his lashings.

"There's plenty of this cord left," declared Tom. "We'll fix up our black friend."

"Do not use that word, Senor," implored Nicolas. "He is *no* good! He is scoundrel! He call me Greaser, an' I will keeck off his head for eet!"

"Wait until we get him tied," Tom proposed.

Sambo, by this time, had gained strength enough to sit up. He was wondering whether he could rise to his feet and sprint away from this dangerous little fury of a Mexican.

"Wait, you black cloud!" cried Nicolas. "I will put you down again!"

"Yo' get away from me——please do!" begged Sambo, recoiling in terror.

"Sambo," laughed Tom, "Africa shouldn't have stirred up Mexico as you did. Now, lie down on your face, place your hands behind you, and I will persuade him to let you alone."

Sambo hesitated.

"Let me at him, Senor!" begged Nicolas, maneuvering forward, his right hand ready. "He is *no* good, I tell you! But I feex him!"

With a yell Sambo Ebony flopped over on his face, placing his hands behind his back.

"Let him alone, Nicolas, as long as he minds," ordered Reade, catching the excited Mexican by the collar. "Only, if he shows signs of making trouble then sail into him fast."

No sign of trouble, however, was there in Sambo. He lay as meek as a lamb while Tom used a lot of the spare cord in taking sundry hitches around the negro's wrists.

"I don't believe he'll get out of that," said Reade grimly, "Now, we'll fix his feet."

This, too, was done, and Sambo lay helpless on the ground.

"You'll make a fine-looking jailbird, my friend," mocked Tom, looking down at the prisoner. "Nor did any man ever better deserve the striped suit that the State of Alabama will present you. Now, Nicolas, I'll stay and watch this black treasure while you run and find help."

"Senor, you go yourself," begged the Mexican. "The men will obey you more queeckly than they would me."

"Oh, you find some of the men and tell 'em to come here to get the fellow who has been blowing up the wall, and they'll come fast enough," smiled Tom.

"But, Senor, suppose thees scoundrel free himself?"

"I won't let him, Nicolas."

"But eef he do?" persisted the Mexican. "Then, as I have shown you, Senor, I can take fine care of heem!"

"There's something in that, too," laughed Tom. "Nicolas, I don't believe it will be risking you any if I leave you here. Besides, I won't have to be gone very long."

"If this black scoundrel he get restless, Senor, I will amuse heem with my forefinger."

Sambo groaned; Nicolas grinned.

"All right," Tom Reade laughed. "I'll be back as soon as I can."

Away he raced at a dog-trot, chuckling. The contrast between bulky Sambo and little Nicolas and the big negro's comic fear of the slim little fellow kept Reade laughing.

"But where on earth did Nicolas learn that trick?" Tom wondered. "I shall have to get him to show it to me. Plainly that trick is worth more than all the muscle that I spent so many years in piling on."

Tom headed his course for the shore end of the wall. Here he would find men in abundance. Moreover, now that the big black was a prisoner the men would hardly be needed on the wall.

"I think I know just how Sambo worked it, too," the engineer reflected, as he ran. "He swam out into the Gulf, towing that little scow behind him. Neither his black head nor the little scow would be seen far on the water on a dark night. Sambo, when he got near enough, could take one of the metal tubes, swim in under water to some point where no watchman was near, and stick the tube fast into the wall. Then another tube, and another——all under water where they would not show to a passing watchman.

"Then, when he had all in place, and while no patrolling watchman was too near, Sambo could begin to attach the wires. That would take but a few minutes. Whenever any one came too near Sambo had but to swim out a little way and tread water until he could return to his job. When, at last, all was complete, Sambo would attach a wire from the bombs to a wire moored at a stated point under water, and then swim in, work his magneto, and touch the whole thing off from a safe hiding place on shore. The explosion itself would shatter the last length of wire. Oh, but it was all slick and easy!"

Not increasing his speed, but keeping steadily at the jog-trot, Tom was at last near enough to the wall to raise his voice and shout.

"Hullo!" came back the answer.

"This is Reade, the chief engineer," Tom answered, through the night. "We've caught the fellow that has been blowing up the wall. A half a dozen of you men hurry over here with your lanterns. Come on the run."

The man who had answered summoned several of his comrades as quickly as he could. As the men had to come in from the wall, however, it took a little time. Then six men reported, almost breathless, to Reade. Still behind them came Corbett on the run, summoned from the boat.

"What's this I hear, Mr. Reade?" puffed the foreman. "You've solved the mystery and caught the fellow who has been dynamiting the wall?"

"Got him and he's tied up, waiting for his ride to jail," Tom chuckled.

"How did it happen, sir?" asked Corbett, staring with his eyes very wide open.

"I caught the fellow——a huge giant of a negro, the same fellow who got Hazelton the other night," replied Tom. "But before the fight was over the black 'got' me, instead, and had me tied up. Then Nicolas came along and put the negro out of the fight, and——"

"Nicolas?" demanded Foreman Corbett incredulously.

"Yes. Nicolas proved himself to be the most fiery little bunch of fighting material that I have ever seen," laughed Reade, as they walked rapidly along.

"How could that Mexican wallop a giant?"

"I'll ask Nicolas to show you, to-morrow," Tom laughed mischievously. "But, Corbett, I believe that four bombs are even now attached to some part of the retaining wall, ready to be set off.

"Great Scott!"

"They won't be set off, though," continued Reade. "I found the firing magneto, and had a chance to cut the wires."

The foreman wanted to ask more questions, while the half dozen workmen trudged along close at their heels, eager to hear every word. Tom, however, suggested that they save their breath in the interest of speed, until they had Mr. Sambo Ebony in safe custody.

"Here we come, Nicolas!" Tom called, as the party neared the spot where captor and captive had been left.

There was no response.

"Nicolas!" Tom called again, with a start.

Still no answer.

"I don't like the look of that," Reade uttered. "Let's get there on the sprint!"

Tom himself caught at one of the lanterns, leading the way. Neither the negro nor the Mexican was where the young chief engineer had left them.

Feverishly, Tom began to search the ground, holding his lantern close.

"Hang the luck!" he quivered, pointing to fragments of cord on the sand. "That negro simply burst his bonds—-and now where is he? Where is Nicolas, for that matter? I thought the little fellow, with his trick, could easily take care of the big black."

But, though they spread out and searched, there was no sign of either the negro or the little brown man.

"I can't understand what has happened," quivered Tom Reade, thinking more of the staunch little Mexican than of the loss of the prisoner.

CHAPTER XVI

A TEST OF REAL NERVE

"What an idiot I was not to stop to consider that Sambo Ebony could snap those cords!" groaned Tom, staring disconcertedly about him. "Yet, if Nicolas were safe I wouldn't so much mind the escape of the black. I shall see him again, and I shall know him wherever I see him."

"Let's look for the trail," proposed Foreman Corbett, holding one of the lanterns close to the ground.

The trail, however, was easy neither to distinguish nor to follow.

"We may as well leave here and search farther," concluded the young engineer. "Before we go, though, we'll get the magneto and take it with us."

Then the procession turned toward the land end of the retaining wall.

"If Nicolas doesn't show up soon," Tom murmured to the foreman, "I shall notify the Blixton police and offer a reward for news of him. That little fellow is too faithful to be left to his fate."

"What would the negro want of Nicolas?" queried the foreman.

"Revenge," Tom replied. "It makes a big bully like him furious to be handled the way Nicolas treated him. But I can't understand how Nicolas failed to repeat his clever trick with the black."

Arrived at the water front the magneto was dumped into the motor boat.

"Seems to me I would smash that thing all to pieces," Suggested Foreman Corbett. "It has done harm enough around this wall."

"I don't believe in destroying anything that is useful," Reade answered, shaking his head. "Besides, we are going to capture Sambo yet, and then we shall want that magneto for evidence."

"What are you going to do to find Nicolas?" Corbett wanted to know.

"I wish I had even an idea," Tom sighed. "Corbett, I wish you would hurry over to Blixton and rout out the police. I've an idea that Sambo may have a hiding place in the town. Nicolas, too, may have been taken that way. I'll sit down and write out a good description of the rascal."

This Reade did, handing the paper to the foreman.

"Who'll take charge here? Corbett asked.

"I will, until you get back, but hurry."

As soon as the foreman had gone Tom stepped into the motor boat, taking the wheel.

"Tune up the engine, Conlon," Reade directed the engine tender. "I'm going to take a run around to the west side of the wall. I'm going to try to find the tubes of high explosive that I'm satisfied were planted in the wall."

"That's a fine job for a dark night, sir," grumbled Conlon. "Suppose we run into the bombs, and they prove to be contact exploders, too?"

"That's one of the risks of the business," Tom retorted grimly.

Before the motor boat had gone far Tom called one of the men aboard to take the wheel. Then the young chief engineer began to experiment with the searchlight.

"What's the idea, sir?" asked Conlon, looking on.

"I want to depress the light, so that we can use it to look down into the water."

"And try to find the bombs?"

"Exactly," Reade nodded.

"Lucky if we don't find the bombs with the keel of the boat," observed Conlon.

Tom succeeded in rigging the light so that he could use it. By the time that the boat was around at the west side of the retaining wall Tom ordered the boat in close alongside. Then, with the depressed searchlight he discovered that he could see the sides of the wall to a depth of some eight feet under the surface.

"That may be enough for our needs," Reade murmured. "Now, run the boat along, slowly and close. I want to scan every bit of the wall."

Less than five minutes later Tom Reade, one hand controlling the searchlight and peering steadily into the water, sang out:

"Stop! Back her——slowly. There, come back five feet. So! Hold her steady!"

As the engine stopped Conlon stepped forward, kneeling by Reade's side.

"There are the bombs, man!" cried Tom exultantly. "See them——the two upper ones?"

"I see something that gleams," admitted Conlon.

"Well, we'll have them up and aboard in a hurry. Then you'll see just what they are."

"You're not going to try to raise the things with the boathook, are you?" queried the engine tender, a look of alarm in his eyes.

"That might be risky," admitted Reade. "I'll go over the side after them and bring them up.

"Don't, Mr. Reade!" urged Conlon with a shiver. "That'll be worse still. You're likely to blow yourself into the next world!"

"I think not——hope not, anyway," answered Tom steadily. "Have you a pair of pliers in your tool box that'll cut small wires?"

"Yes," replied Conlon.

"Get them for me."

Reade removed his coat, shoes and socks, then took the pliers.

"Let one of the men jump ashore with the boathook and hold the boat steady," was Reade's next direction.

This being done, Reade deflected the searchlight for one more look into the water. Then, the pliers in his right hand, he mounted to the rail of the boat.

"Be careful, sir——do," begged Conlon. "What I'm afraid of is that the bombs are contact exploders."

"It's likely," nodded Reade. "I'll be as careful as I can."

Tom did not dive; the distance was too short. Instead, he let himself down into the water slowly. Then his head vanished beneath the surface of the water.

"Whew! The nerve of that young fellow!", thought Conlon with shuddering admiration.

"Ob co'se Massa Reade done got nerve," nodded the negro at the wheel. "Dat's one reason why, Misto Conlon, Massa Reade is boss."

"There are other reasons why he's boss," grunted the engine tender. "Mr. Reade has nerve, but he also has brains in his head. Any man with brains and the sense to use 'em goes to the top, while I stay down a good deal lower, and you, Rastus, are still lower."

"Ah reckon Ah got a two-bit hat on top o' only two cents' wo'th o' brains, Misto Conlon," grinned the darkey.

Conlon was an Irishman, and naturally, therefore, no coward. Yet with the possibility that Tom would run afoul of a contact-exploding bomb and send them all skyward, the engine tender waited at the rail with drawn breath.

Finally, there was a ripple on the water. Then Tom's head appeared; next his shoulders.

"Conlon!"

"Here, sir."

"Here is one of the bombs. Handle it carefully."

"Trust me, sir."

Conlon drew the metal tube, with a piece of wire pendant from it, as carefully as though it had been a royal baby and heir to a throne. Into the boat the engine tender lifted the thing, and laid it carefully in a locker. By the time that Conlon was back at the rail Reade had gone below again.

"Down dere, aftah mo' death!" grinned the darkey. A colored man can usually be brave when serving under a white leader in whom he has full confidence.

Presently Tom came up with another metal tube, like the first.

"I'll hang on and get my breath," Tom informed the men in the boat, as he rested one hand on the rail. "The other two bombs are about three feet lower, and it's going to be hard to work at the lower depth."

"Be careful, won't you, sir?" urged Conlon, in a somewhat awed voice. "Mr. Reade, we can't afford to lose you until this job is completed. Men with all the nerve you show are scarce in the world."

"I know where there are forty thousand men with at least as much nerve, many of them having several times as much as I," laughed Tom.

"Where on earth are they?" demanded the Irishman.

"In the United States Navy. If there were a battleship here the jackies would be fighting for the honor of going down after these bombs."

Then Reade dropped out of sight, once more. Nor was it long before he had the third and the fourth bombs aboard the boat. Then he climbed in himself, dripping like a shaggy Newfoundland dog.

"Put in at the dock now," the young chief ordered, and the boat started on its way.

"Some one signaling from the wall lower down," Tom soon informed the negro pilot. "Put in where you see the signaling."

"It is I, Corbett," called the foreman of that name. "Mr. Reade, these two men with me belong to the Blixton police."

"Perhaps you had rather walk down to the dock, then, instead of getting into the boat," laughed Reade. "We have four bombs aboard, just taken out of the wall above here."

Accordingly the three turned and walked. At the landing the policemen gazed curiously at the bombs.

"Do you want to take charge of these?" Reade queried.

"Not particular about it," replied the policeman, with a shrug. "We'd be scorched for endangering the town if we took those things into Blixton. Your foreman, Mr. Reade, called us out here to see if we could get trail of your missing Mexican servant."

"That's a vastly more important thing to do," Tom replied with enthusiasm. "I want to find Nicolas before I do another thing."

"Come here, Bill," called one of the officers.

Out of the shadows near the shore came a youth leading a dog on a leash.

"This dog is a bloodhound," announced one of the policemen with visible pride. "Take him to where the scent of the Mexican starts, and the dog will follow as long as there's any scent left. But, first, we'll have to have something that the Mexican has worn, so that the hound will know the true scent."

"That will take but a few minutes," declared Reade energetically. "Come up to the house, and I'll find something that Nicolas has worn."

69

Corbett remained behind to take care of the bombs. Tom led the officers and the youth with the hound on a brisk walk up to the house.

"Wait out here," murmured Tom, "and I'll bring something out. If we all go into the house we'll wake my partner, Hazelton, and he has enough work to do in the daytime, without being kept up at night."

While the others remained outside Tom stole into the house. There was a room in the rear, off the kitchen, where Nicolas slept. Into that room Reade stepped noiselessly.

It was not necessary to strike a match, for, in the very faint light there, Tom espied an object on the foot of the bed that he recognized——one of the Mexican's white canvas shoes.

Tom snatched it up quickly. Then, despite his steady nerves, he staggered back.

CHAPTER XVII

TOM MAKES AN UNEXPECTED CAPTURE

For an unearthly scream pierced the air. There was a wrench, a bounding figure——and then Tom Reade felt a jolt near his solar plexus that made him gasp.

"Stop that!" gasped the young chief engineer.

"You, Senor?" demanded an incredible, drowsy voice.

"Yes; it's I——Reade."

"A thousand pardons, Senor!"

"So this is you, Nicolas?"

"Yes, Senor."

"What are you doing here?"

"The negro got away from me."

"I know that, but——"

"I could not help it, Senor. I assure you I was not careless."

"I never knew you to be careless, Nicolas."

"Thank you, Senor. But I stood over that black scoundrel, watching for the slightest move on his part. I had my forefinger ready, and he did not dare move."

"I can quite believe that," agreed Tom, dryly, "after the poke you just gave me."

"Again a thousand pardons, Senor, but in the dark, and awaking so suddenly, I did not see you or know you."

"I can quite believe that, Nicolas."

"As I was saying, Senor, I was watching over the black man when some one came up behind me——so softly that I did not hear. But I felt. *Ah!* What I felt! It was a fist that seemed to break in the top of my head. Down I went, and I heard a voice. I knew that voice, too. So would you have known it, Senor!"

"Whose voice was it?" asked Tom, curiously.

"The voice of Evarts."

"The discharged foreman?"

"Yes, Senor. But I am delaying my story. While Evarts was speaking I heard another sound. At one effort the negro snapped the cords that held him. Ah, he is a powerful brute."

"He is," Tom affirmed solemnly.

"I knew it was my task to keep the negro from getting away," continued the little Mexican excitedly. "So I leaped up, extended my forefinger and rushed at him. But thees Evarts——hees feest catch me between the eyes. I do not have to guess the spot where he struck me, Senor, for I can feel it yet. Down I went, and knew no more. When next I opened my eyes I found myself lying in the middle of a theecket of bushes. I theenk, perhaps, the scoundrels believed they had killed me, and so they hid my body. But I have fool' them. I am still alive——much alive!"

"What did you do when you came to, Nicolas?"

"Senor," protested the Mexican, "there was no more need of me. You had gone after men. Eef you came back, you have many men with you, so you do not need me. For that reason I come home."

Even in the dark the young engineer could "feel" Nicolas's shudder. Tom could not repress a smile that threatened to become a chuckle.

"I was varee sleepy," continued Nicolas, "and so I lay down. I forgot to undress, or even to take off my shoes. I fall asleep, and I dream much. I see the big negro again, and I dream that I have more fight with heem. Then, when you pull my foot, I wake up in one gr-rand sweat, for I theenk the big black attack me once more. I am glad——so glad that it is not true."

"Nicolas," cried Tom, "you have done fighting enough for one night. Yet tell me, how did you happen to be at hand to-night in time to save me from Mr. Sambo Ebony?"

"Because I see you start away to-night," replied Nicolas, "an' I see that you go alone. I know that you mos' likely run into trouble, an' so I follow you. Sure enough, Senor, you find trouble——and I heet heem with my finger!"

"You surely did 'hit him with your finger,' Nicolas," laughed Tom, grasping the little Mexican's hand and wringing it. "But now come outside. I had sent for the police to find you, and now I must show them that you are already found."

Together they went out on the porch. Tom explained the situation.

"Then you don't need us, after all?" asked one of the policemen.

"Not to find Nicolas," Tom Reade admitted. "But do you know Evarts?"

"Used to be your foreman?"

"Yes."

"We know him," nodded the policeman.

"Then," Reade continued, "I wish you would search through Blixton for him. If you find him, be good enough to lock him up and notify me."

"Is there a warrant out against him?" asked one of the policemen, cautiously.

"You don't need one," Tom replied. "I will make a charge of felony against Evarts, to the effect that he is concerned in the outrages against our wall. On a felony charge you don't need a warrant. Then, too, try to find the big negro."

"What's his name?"

"I don't know his name," Tom answered. "I've dubbed him 'Sambo Ebony.' You have the description of him that I wrote out. Arrest Sambo, by all means, if you can find him, and I'll make a felony charge against him, too. The negro is the one who has been blowing up the sea wall."

71

"We'll look for the pair all through the town, Mr. Reade," promised the officers.

"Do! And, on behalf of the company, I'll offer a two-hundred dollar reward for the arrest of each man!"

With that prospect to spur them on the policemen hastened away, followed by the young man with the bloodhound.

"Now, Nicolas," pressed Reade, turning around at the faithful little brown man, "you tumble back into bed."

"But you, Senor?"

"Don't worry about me. I've probably done all I need to do to-night. I shall probably sit here on the porch and think until daylight. Then I'll call Hazelton, and go to bed for a few hours' sleep before I appear in court against the gamblers and the bootleggers. Go to bed, Nicolas, and sleep! That's an order, remember!"

The Mexican therefore went to his bedroom without protest. Presently Reade became aware of the fact that his clothing had not by any means fully dried. He went to his room, took a vigorous rub-down, donned dry clothing, and then went out on the porch.

Though the night was dark the air was delicious. The combined odors of many flowers came in on the faintly stirring breeze.

Tom leaned back in a chair, his feet on the porch railing. His senses lulled by the quiet and repose of the night he was in danger of falling asleep.

Of a sudden he came to with a start. Off among the trees to the eastward, near the road, a human being was stirring.

Reade rose, moving swiftly back more into the shadow. Then he watched, every sense alert. Yes; some one was moving, out there amid the trees. What he could not see, Tom discovered by his acute sense of hearing.

"I'll put a hot pebble in that fellow's bonnet, whoever he is!" Tom muttered vengefully. Entering the house, he left at the rear, then made a stealthy, roundabout trip that brought him at the farther edge of the litte grove of trees.

Now the young engineer crouched close to the ground as he listened. Once more he heard that some one moving, not many yards away. It was pitch-black in there amid the trees. Guided by his ears, Tom moved closer and closer without making a betraying sound. Suddenly he found the tall figure looming up almost in his path.

"Now, I've got you!" cried Tom exultantly, making a bound that should have carried his hands to the throat of the prowler.

But the other, like a flash, went on the defensive. Tom felt himself parried, then clutched at. The next instant the prowler had the young engineer in a tackle that carried Tom Reade back to the good old high school days at home. The young engineer was dumped on the ground as though he had been a sack of flour.

"Great Scott!" quivered Tom Reade. "No one but Dick Prescott ever had that tackle down fine!"

"Well, you blithering idiot!" came the indignant answer. "That's who I am—- Prescott!"

CHAPTER XVIII
THE ARMY "ON THE JOB"

"You, Dick?" gasped Tom, stumbling ruefully to his feet. Then he leaped at his late foe, throwing his arms around him. The two fairly hugged each other, Yes; here was Dick Prescott, not so many weeks a graduate of the Military Academy at West Point, and now, if you please, Second Lieutenant Richard Prescott, United States Army!

"Well, of all the strange things that the Illinois Central Railroad brings into Alabama!" grunted Tom, now gripping Dick by the hand and holding on as though he never meant to let go.

"If the Illinois Central had built its tracks through to Blixton I probably would have arrived at a civilized hour," laughed Dick. "As it was, I had to come in on a wood-burning, backwoods road and the train was only five hours and a half behind schedule. Then, from a sleepy policeman I got directions that enabled me to find this place after an hour's hard work." To what effect? Only to be pounced upon by you as though you had caught me in the act of stealing all the water in the Gulf of Mexico!"

"Stop your roasting," laughed Tom joyfully. "But say, it *does* seem good to set eyes on you again, after two years."

All of our readers who have read the "*High School Boys Series*" and the "*West Point Series*" know all about Dick Prescott, the famous leader of Dick & Co.

"What are you now?" Tom asked eagerly. "A general, or only a colonel?"

"Nothing but a shavetail," laughed Dick. "Shavetail is the army nickname for a second lieutenant."

"I've got to join my regiment, the Thirty-fourth Infantry, out in Colorado very soon," continued Prescott. "But I came down here to spend a few days with you, if you can stand me."

"If we can stand you!" chuckled Tom, patting his old high school chum on the back. "Say, where's Greg?"

Greg Holmes had been another member of Dick & Co., and Dick's chum and comrade at West Point.

"Well, you see," laughed Lieutenant Prescott, "Greg has been falling in love with six girls a year regularly ever since he entered West Point. Now that he's in the army he has started in to increase the yearly average. He's visiting a Miss Deering, who lives near Chicago."

"Greg's likely never to marry," wisely remarked Tom. "These fellows who catch a new love fever every few weeks always end up by finding that no girl wants them. But say, Dick you hardly look the soldier."

"Why not?"

"Well, one would expect to see an army officer in uniform, you know."

"An officer rarely travels in uniform, unless on duty with troops," explained Dick.

"How did you like West Point?"

"Fine!" said Dick, grimly. "It was like four years in prison, only more so. When I look back I shudder at the incessant grind I had to endure there. Yet I'm

73

going to be happy, now I'm through, for I couldn't be happy anywhere except in the United States Army."

"What crazy notions some folks have of happiness," murmured Tom, mockingly. "However, old fellow, we're not going to fight, are we? Now, hustle over to the house. Harry is sleeping at the present moment, but I won't let him have a wink more of sleep to-night. It's getting toward daylight, anyway, and too much sleep isn't good for a fellow. But don't talk above a whisper, Dick, when we get near the house. I don't want Harry, by any chance, to catch a sound of your voice until he comes out on the porch and runs into you."

Chatting away in low tones the two old-time high school chums gained the porch.

"Now, just stay here," whispered Tom, then strode into the house. He entered his partner's room, gripping the slumber-seized Hazelton with a strong clasp.

"Oh, quit your fooling!" protested a sleepy voice from the pillow.

"Time to get up, you slant-eyed rations stealer!" muttered Tom gruffly. "Come on. You're needed, and there's no time to be lost. Up with you!"

Tom dragged his drowsy partner from the bed, seating him on the edge of it.

"Now, shed your pajamas and pull on something decent," Reade commanded grimly. "Hustle! There's a conference going on outside, and you're wanted. Hurry! Want me to dump the pitcher of water on you? I'll do it if you give your eyes another rub!"

Hazelton was now fully convinced that something important was in the air. If not, he knew that his chum never would have hauled him out of bed in the darkest hours of the night.

"If you throw any water I'll shave you with the bread-knife," retorted Harry. "But you can keep on talking to me, so that I won't fall asleep while I'm trying to dress."

Slowly, at first, then more rapidly, Hazelton got his clothes on. Pouring water into the basin he sopped a towel in it, then liberally applied it to his face. The water waked him rapidly.

"Now, lead me forth to where duty calls," mimicked Harry.

"Run along out on to the porch," ordered Tom. "I'll be there in a moment."

Still yawning, Hazelton groped his way out into the hall, along the dark passage, and thence out into the night. Some one stood there, and Harry walked curiously toward him.

"Howdy, whoever you are," was Hazelton's greeting.

"Halloo, Harry, old chum," came Dick Prescott's laughing answer.

"Dick Prescott!" gasped Harry delightedly.

"I suppose you think I might have waited until daylight," laughed Dick, as their hands met.

"I'm heartily glad you didn't wait," said Harry. "How long can you stay with us?"

"Not as long as I'd like to, for I'm due at Fort Clowdry in a very few days."

"And Greg?"

Lieutenant Prescott gave the same explanation he had furnished Tom.

"How does it seem to be an army officer?" Harry continued.

"I believe it to be the finest career on earth," Prescott answered. "Still, as you can guess, I'm utterly without experience so far. After a few days more I shall have my first day as an officer on duty with troops. But do you and Tom continue to find engineering the grandest career on earth?"

"We certainly do," affirmed Hazelton.

"It must be very interesting," agreed Dick. "Still, I imagine there is yet enough of the primitive savage in the average man to make him enjoy a real fight once in a while. That's an experience you're denied in your calling, but an army officer may always look forward to the chance of seeing a little fighting."

Hazelton glanced humorously at his partner before he replied:

"At present there's a very good chance of a fight right here at this camp."

"So?" Dick Prescott asked, sitting up with a look of interest.

"Not so much chance as there was," said Tom gravely. "The fight came off to-night. Harry, I met the big black—caught him redhanded."

"You did?" cried Hazelton, leaping up. "And you never called me?"

"There wasn't any chance," Tom assured him. "The meeting and the fight didn't take place on this porch."

Tom now had two very interested auditors. For Prescott's benefit Reade first sketched a brief outline of the troubles that had led up to the present, including an account of the wrecking of substantial portions of the retaining wall. Then he came down to the events of the night.

"Oh, and I had to miss it," sighed Harry, disappointedly. "I'd have missed a week of sleep just to have been in to-night's doings. And, if I had been with you, Tom, we'd now have Mr. Sambo Ebony in jail."

"I think we've blocked the black rascal's game on the wall, anyway," said Tom.

"There's just a fair chance that you haven't yet blocked it," remarked the young army officer thoughtfully. "Of course this Sambo of yours merely represents a well-organized gang. This gang may have more ways than one of damaging the property of the Melliston Company. From all I can see, Tom and Harry, you're likely to need to be more vigilant than ever. Whew! But I'm glad that I can be with you a few days. I'm likely to come in for a choice lot of excitement. Also, I may very likely be able to help out a lot."

"We wouldn't put you to that trouble, Dick," protested Tom. "You're to be our guest—not our policeman."

"Are you going to try to keep me out of all the excitement and fun?" Lieutenant Dick demanded, indignantly. "Sleep? Can't I get enough of that when I go aboard a Pullman again and am riding out to Colorado? Of course I'm going to help—and I'm going to have my share of all the opportunities for excitement here—or else I'm going to cut your acquaintance."

"Why, of course we'll be delighted to have your help, Dick, if you want to stand the racket," Reade made haste to say. "It will surely seem like doubling—or trebling—our forces, to have Dick Prescott working hand in hand with us."

"Then that's settled," cried Dick, with an air of satisfaction.

"You haven't had any sleep lately, have you, Dick?" inquired Tom, after they had chatted a little longer.

"No; I haven't."

"Then you must turn in and get a few hours," proposed Reade. "I must have a little myself, as I shall have to be up and go into court during the coming forenoon."

"I'm wide awake now," said Harry. "So I'll sit right here on the porch and dream of Dick and Greg, and good old Dave Darrin and Danny Dalzell, and the good times we had in old Gridley. What time do you want to be up, Tom?"

"Not later than eight," Reade answered.

"Trust me," said Harry promptly. Harry went to his own bedroom, pulled his bed apart, remade it with fresh linen, and with a final grip of Dick's hand, he left the army officer to turn in there.

At eight o'clock Hazelton called both Tom and Dick. They turned out promptly, to find that Nicolas had laid an appetizing breakfast on the porch.

Then Tom had to hurry over to Blixton, Dick going with him, while Hazelton went down to the breakwater to superintend the day's work there.

Only a little time had to be spent in the justice's stuffy court. Hawkins and his fellow gamblers and bootleggers were arraigned and held in one thousand dollars' bail each for trial. As none of them had the money the eight men were sent to the county jail pending trial.

"That's queer," mused Tom, aloud, as he and Dick walked back to camp. "You'd think that professional gamblers would have money enough to put up small bail."

"Not if they're working for other people," suggested Dick. "These men may be merely the agents of some larger crowd."

"Meaning that the larger crowd may be a sort of vice trust, operating in many fields at the same time?" queried Reade.

"Something of the sort," replied the young army officer. "To-day nearly everything has been capitalized on a large scale of combined capital. Why shouldn't vice be?"

"I begin to think you're more than half right in your guess," Tom admitted. "Your explanation is about the only way to account for a fellow like Hawkins not having a thousand at his instant disposal. However, if these fellows represent a vice trust, then I suppose it will be a question of only a little time when the trust sends down money enough to put up the needed bail."

"That will undoubtedly happen," nodded Dick. "And then you'll have to look out for that fellow, Hawkins, and all the men he can command. Hawkins looked at you, in court, as though he'd enjoy pulverizing you."

"I'm ready, when he is," laughed Tom. "If he'd only fight in the open I wouldn't be at all afraid of him."

Tom now led the way down to the retaining wall. Prescott gazed with great interest at the signs of activity. On a closer inspection he was even more interested. He was capable of understanding very fully what was being done here, for every graduate of the United States Military Academy is supposed to be a capable engineer.

"You've a difficult task on hand, but your basic principle is sound, and you're doing the work finely and economically," Dick declared with emphasis.

Harry came in from the outer end of the wall and joined them. He listened with pride to the praises that the army officer showered on the engineers.

"I wish Mr. Bascomb, the president of the company, could hear you," said Harry. "He isn't altogether sure that we know what we're about in anything that we're doing."

"Then I've a very good mental picture of Bascomb," declared Dick, bluntly. "Bascomb is something of a chump. By the way, if you want to get square with Mr. Bascomb, why don't you coax him down here to help you look out for the evil-doers who are combined against you?"

"He wouldn't be much use," sighed Tom. "He's an impossible sort of chap. He wanted us to stop our crusade against camp vice. Said it was hurting business."

"What craft is that?" inquired Dick, looking toward a sailboat that was moving lazily along about a half-mile to the eastward.

"I don't know," Tom answered, after a look. "Never saw the boat before. Regular cabin cruiser, isn't she, about forty feet long?"

"About that," nodded Dick. "What interested me in her was the fact that a fellow on board has been watching us with a marine glass. I caught the glint of the sun on the lenses."

"Why should he want to be watching us?" demanded Hazelton.

"That's just what made me curious," replied Prescott. "As an army officer, if this were a fort that I commanded in troublous times, I'd want to look into any strange craft that I caught cruising lazily in the offing and holding a marine glass on us."

"I wonder if that boat can be in the service of those who are annoying us?" Tom muttered.

"It's an even chance that it is a 'hostile ship,'" Prescott suggested. "You have a motor boat here. I'm inclined to think you ought to use it in overhauling that suspicious craft. Of course you'd have no right unless there was a police officer along. Can you get one?"

"The authorities in Blixton would send a policeman on request."

"Then send a messenger to request them to send over a policeman in citizen's clothes," proposed Dick.

Tom promptly despatched Foreman Dill on that errand.

"Now don't let the men on the boat see that you're paying any more attention," Prescott advised. "Leave it to me, and I'll contrive to keep the boat and its people under observation without looking too plainly in their direction."

In due time the plain clothes policeman arrived. He, the young engineers and the army lieutenant boarded the "Morton," which put out from the landing as though on a trip of inspection of the wall.

"Don't anyone look over at the sloop," Prescott urged. "I'll do the watching. A fellow on that craft is holding the glasses on us right now. Officer, do you demand the assistance of all present in any police duty that may come up?"

"I do," replied the Blixton policeman, a man named Carnes, returning Prescott's wink.

"All right, then," laughed Dick. "That demand makes policemen of us all. Tom, you can turn, now, when ready, and put on full speed in going after that craft."

Reade gave the order for full speed, then took the steering wheel himself.

"Guilty conscience!" laughed Prescott. "There's the sloop putting about at once and heading away from us."

"They can't get away from us, in this light wind," chuckled the young chief engineer.

A few minutes later the "Morton" came up within easy hailing distance of the sloop, aboard which only one man now appeared.

"Sloop ahoy!" called the policeman. "What are you doing in these waters?"

"Looking for a good fishing ground," answered the dark-faced man at the tiller.

"Then you're too far in by some three miles," answered the policeman.

"Thank you, cap'n," acknowledged the sailing master of the sloop.

"You're welcome," the policeman continued, "but ease off your sheet and lay to. We want to come aboard."

"You can't!" flatly retorted the skipper.

"You're wrong there," retorted the policeman. "This is a police party, and I tell you that we are coming aboard. Lay to, or we shall have to start a lot of trouble for you."

In the policeman's hand suddenly glistened a revolver. Tom ran the motor boat close alongside. With a snarl the man left off his sheet. The policeman and Dick Prescott leaped aboard the craft, Tom and Harry following.

"This is a cheeky outrage!" snarled the skipper, scowling at the invaders.

"Then keep the change, and welcome," laughed the policeman, taking his stand close to the skipper.

Dick Prescott made a dive at the cabin door, which was closed.

"Open this door!" he summoned.

As the door did not open Dick placed his shoulder against it.

"Open the door, or I'll break it down," Dick insisted.

There was still no answer. Thereupon Prescott proceeded to put his threat into execution. Harry bounded forward to help. Under their combined assault the door gave way.

Lieutenant Prescott was the first to enter the dark little cabin. Poor as the light was his eyes caught sight of something that made him gasp.

"This is the big capture of the season!" cried Dick jubilantly.

CHAPTER XIX

A NEW MYSTERY PEEPS IN

"Get out of here, or you'll get something you don't want," roared an ugly voice at the farther end of the cabin.

At sound of that voice Tom Reade started. He thrust his head in the open doorway.

"Hullo, Evarts!" called the young chief engineer.

"Get out of here!" came the furious order.

"So you've openly joined the enemy, Evarts?" demanded Tom, as his eyes fell upon the object that had first claimed Lieutenant Dick Prescott's attention.

"You've no business here! Get out, or I'll shoot," cried Evarts, defiantly.

"Don't be too quick on the shoot," warned the Blixton policeman, who still had his own revolver in his hand. "This is a police party, and you're under arrest. Start any shooting trouble, and the air will be full of it."

"Clear out, and I'll come outside and talk with you," proposed Evarts, for it really was the discharged foreman.

"All right," nodded the policeman. "Gentlemen, let him step outside."

The others left the entrance to the cabin, As Evarts, his pistol now back in his pocket, stepped sullenly outside, Harry Hazelton dropped back into the doorway.

"Glad to meet you, Mr. Evarts," grinned the police officer, deftly slipping handcuffs on the fellow's wrists.

"This is treachery!" stormed the prisoner. "I didn't surrender to you. I only came out to talk with you."

"If you didn't surrender, then excuse me, and go ahead and put up a fight," laughed the policeman, handily removing Evarts's revolver from a hip pocket.

"Now, look in here, Tom," urged Dick. "Do you see what caught my eye?"

Prescott pointed to a sharp-nosed cylinder, some eight feet long. Just as it lay the propeller at the other end was invisible to one at the doorway of the cabin.

"It's a home-made imitation of a Whitehead torpedo," Lieutenant Dick went on, in explanation. "If it proves to be charged with explosives then the mere having of it aboard this sloop will prove embarrassing to these two prisoners to explain in court. If it isn't loaded, that will be almost as bad, as such a torpedo can be rather easily loaded, and then set in operation by clock-work machinery that will control the propeller."

"Young man, you seem to think you know a good deal about torpedoes," sneered Evarts.

"He ought to," Harry retorted quietly. "He's a West Point man and an army officer. Therefore, he's a specialist in some kinds of explosives."

Evarts's face turned somewhat paler at this information of having an army officer on hand as a witness.

"Do you call me a prisoner, too?" asked the man at the tiller uneasily.

"Something like it, I guess," nodded Dick.

"Say, but that's a pretty rank deal against an honest man," protested the skipper hoarsely. "I hired this boat out to that man, the one you call Evarts, but I didn't know what he was up to."

"You didn't know that torpedoes are used for wicked work either, eh?" pressed Lieutenant Dick.

"I'll swear that I didn't know what it was that he brought on board," cried the skipper. "Evarts said it was a new device for killing fish at wholesale."

"You may be telling the truth," Tom broke in.

"I am," declared the skipper eagerly.

"Then explain it to the court," Reade continued. "If you can prove to a judge and a jury that you're an honest man, and always have been one, you may get off on the charge that will be made against you."

"Then you don't believe me?" asked the skipper anxiously.

"It isn't for me to say," Tom replied crisply. "It's a job for a judge and a jury."

"Then I'm to be a prisoner?"

"That's for the policeman here to say."

"You're a prisoner, my man," nodded the policeman. "Now, sail your boat into the landing over yonder."

"Some one else will sail it," retorted the skipper, angrily, as he abandoned his tiller.

"I'll take the tiller," Harry suggested, and did so. He hauled in the sheet, brought the boat around and headed for the landing with the skill of an old sailor.

"My man, since you don't want to sail the boat you'll have to go as a real prisoner," announced the policeman. He produced a pair of handcuffs, snapping them over the man's wrists.

In a short time Harry brought the sailboat up to the landing. The motor boat had followed, but did not come all the way in. After the sail had been lowered and made snug the party took up its way, on foot, to the nearby town of Blixton.

Justice Sampson was found, and consented to open court immediately. Officer Carnes brought his prisoners forward, stating the charge. The young engineers and the army officer gave their testimony.

"The prisoners are held for trial, and bail fixed at five thousand dollars in each case," decided the court.

The torpedo had been left on the sloop, in charge of a foreman. The justice now ordered two officers to go back and bring over the torpedo, which was to be held until a chemist could examine and take samples of whatever explosive might be found inside.

As Dick was a United States Army officer, under orders to proceed to his post within the next few days, the court reduced his testimony to writing, and permitted Prescott to sign this under oath.

It had been a busy forenoon. Now it was time for luncheon, and the three chums returned to the house to eat. In the afternoon they visited the wall, remaining there until four o'clock. On their return to the house Tom and Harry were greeted by Mr. Prenter, who had been waiting for them.

"I heard the news of last night's doings, and to-day's, and came right down," explained the treasurer of the Melliston Company. "Reade, I'm glad to be able to say that you appear to have brought us to the end of the explosion troubles."

"Or else we're just starting with that trouble," Reade smiled wistfully. "Mr. Prenter, I must say that there appears to be no end to the surprises with which our enemies are capable of supplying us."

Tom then nodded to Dick to come forward and presented him to the treasurer.

"An army officer?" asked Mr. Prenter eagerly. "Then I'm doubly glad to meet you, Mr. Prescott. You've seen the breakwater work? As an army officer and an engineer what do you think of it?"

"It's great!" said Dick, though he added laughingly: "Reade and Hazelton are such dear old friends of mine that any testimony in their favor is likely to be charged to friendship."

"I'll believe what an army officer says, even in praise of his best friends," smiled Mr. Prenter.

Foreman Johnson, who had been over in town, now came along. He halted some distance away, beckoning to Reade.

"Mr. Reade," murmured the foreman, in an undertone, "over in Blixton I just heard some news that I thought would interest you. Evarts is out on bail."

"He furnished a five thousand surety?" queried Tom.

"Yes, sir, and who do you suppose went on his bond?"

"I can't imagine who the idiot is."

"The man who signed Evarts's bond," continued Foreman Johnson solemnly, "was Mr. Bascomb, president of this company!"

"Whew!" muttered Tom aghast. "And that's all I've got to say on this subject."

"I thought you'd like to know the news," remarked Johnson, "and so I came to tell you."

"Please accept my thanks," Tom answered. Then, as the foreman passed along, Reade went back to his friends.

"You seem staggered about something," remarked Mr. Prenter, eyeing him keenly.

"Possibly I am," admitted Tom. "Evarts is out on bail."

"Now, what fool or rogue could have signed that fellow's bail bond?" demanded Mr. Prenter in exasperation.

"Careful, sir!" warned Tom smilingly. "I've just been informed that the bail bond was signed by Mr. Bascomb, president of the Melliston Company."

"Well, of all the crazy notions!" gasped Mr. Prenter. "But there! I won't say more. Bascomb is a queer fellow in some things, but he's a good fellow in lots of things, and a square, honest man in all things. If he signed Evarts's bond, there was a reason, and not a dishonest one."

"But Evarts won't behave," predicted Harry dismally. "After all our trouble we shall still have to remain on guard night and day."

"It'll be an airship next," laughed Dick Prescott.

"Unless Sambo Ebony comes forward once more, and finds out how to lay wires by a new submarine route," retorted Tom Reade.

All the present company felt unaccountably gloomy just at this moment. There could be no guessing what would occur next to hamper or destroy the fruits of their hard labor.

CHAPTER XX

A SECRET IN SIGHT

"Mr. Prenter," asked Tom suddenly, "is there anything about which you wish to see me just now?"

"Not particularly," replied the treasurer. "Only, in view of late developments I'm going to remain about for the next few days, unless you order me out of the house. I want to be close to the trouble."

"Then, if I'm not needed," gaped Reade, "I'm going to turn in and steal a little sleep. I need rest."

"As I'm going to stay up to-night, Tom, and keep you company through the dark hours, I'm for the bale of lint, too," announced Lieutenant Prescott.

"At what hour shall I call you?" asked Harry.

"At eight o'clock to-night," answered Tom.

Refreshed by a few hours' sleep Tom and Dick were called, to find their supper ready. Nicolas stood behind their chairs, attentive to their needs.

Mr. Prenter remained out on the porch, but Harry sat at table with his friends.

"Has Mr. Bascomb put in an appearance here?" Tom inquired.

"No," said Hazelton briefly.

"He certainly has wound up my curiosity," murmured Tom. "Why on earth should he bail out Evarts?"

"Probably because Evarts asked him to," suggested Dick.

"But why should he want to please Evarts in such a matter?"

"Well, you know," hinted Harry, "we've heard that Evarts is some sort of relative to Mr. Bascomb."

"But the rascal has been working to ruin this company," Tom protested, "and Mr. Bascomb is the trusted president of the company."

"Yet *is* Mr. Bascomb really fit to be trusted?" Prescott propounded.

"Mr. Prenter seems to think so, and he is a capable judge of men," Tom rejoined. "It is the combination of all these circumstances taken together that makes me so curious over Mr. Bascomb's being willing to bail the fellow."

"Oh, well, it's too much of a puzzle for us," said Harry, shrugging his shoulders. "All we've got to do is to keep our eyes open and faithfully guard the property that is entrusted to our care. However, I'm growing sour and sore. Here I've got to go to bed presently, and you and Dick are going to be prowling about all night. You'll have all the excitement, while I'll be in bed."

"You seem to forget," Tom reminded him, "that the last big excitement took place in the daytime, during your shift. Dick and I may have a lazy night, and you may have the air full of wreckage to-morrow in broad daylight."

They chatted a little while with Mr. Prenter, outside, and then Dick rose at Tom's signal.

"We must be starting," said Reade. "I don't know just what we're going to do to-night, but we have miles to cover I'm afraid."

"Being an army officer, Dick, you've got a pistol, of course," suggested Harry hopefully.

"I've a brace of them," nodded the army man.

"Good!" cheered Harry.

"But both of them, unloaded at that, are in my trunks at Mobile," laughed Dick, whereat Tom chuckled. Harry Hazelton was much inclined to want to carry a pistol in times of danger, but Tom didn't believe in any such habit.

"I thought soldiers went armed," muttered Hazelton ruefully.

"Only when on duty," Dick informed him.

Nicolas wistfully watched Reade out of sight. The Mexican had been ordered to remain at home to-night, and on no account to think of following his employer. That didn't at all agree with the faithful fellow's wishes.

"They'll be sure to get into some trouble, Senor Hazelton," Nicolas said mournfully. "I should be on their flank, watching over them."

"You don't know Gridley boys," laughed Harry, "if you don't understand that Dick Prescott and Tom Reade, together, are a hard team to beat."

In the meantime Tom led the way down to the camp of workmen. Reade stopped to speak with one of his reliable negroes, whom he found softly strumming a banjo under a tree.

"Are there any visitors in camp to-night who shouldn't be here?" asked Tom.

"I doan' beliebe so, boss," replied the colored man. "Dem gamblers an' bootleggers ain' done got bail yet, has they, sah?"

"I don't believe they have," replied Tom. "There are no others of their kind here, then?"

"I doan' beliebe so, sah."

Tom and Dick strolled through the camp, but all was quiet there. Many of the men were outside their shacks or tents, smoking and waiting for turning-in time to come.

"Looks as orderly as a camp-meeting," declared Lieutenant Prescott. "I'm glad to see, Tom, that you're for the decent camp every time."

"The decent camp is the only kind that contains efficient workmen for engineering jobs," Reade answered dryly.

Presently they strolled out of camp, on the farther side. This was what the young engineer really wanted to do—-to vanish suddenly, in a fashion that would not be likely to be noted by hostile eyes. Now Reade and his army chum proceeded softly, and without words. Through the deep woods Tom was heading for the spot where he had found the magneto.

Sambo Ebony was at large, and Tom believed that other things than the magneto had been concealed at this spot. If Sambo intended any further assaults on the retaining wall he would be quite likely to come this way. So here Tom Reade was resolved to remain and watch, even if he had to put in most of the night there.

Behind some bushes he and Dick found a hiding place looking out upon the scene of the late conflict with "Mr. Ebony."

Without even whispered conversation time dragged slowly. More than an hour dragged by, and both watchers were beginning to feel decidedly bored.

At last, however, footsteps came that way. Both watchers crouched lower and waited.

The new-comer approached the place rather uncertainly. At last, however, he stood revealed. Tom Reade felt like yelling in his utter astonishment.

For President Bascomb, of the Melliston Company, now stood before them. After a glance about Mr. Bascomb walked slowly up and down, as though he were waiting for some one.

Dick, of course, did not know Mr. Bascomb. However, as Tom kept silent the young soldier did the same.

"What on earth can Bascomb be doing here?" Tom wondered. "Is he, too, one of the conspirators? It is unbelievable! Yet with what speed he obeyed Evarts's summons to come and bail him out! It makes me feel like a sneak to be here spying on the president of the company that employs me——and yet there's something here that certainly must be looked into!"

Fifteen minutes more dragged by, with Mr. Bascomb walking impatiently back and forth, occasionally heaving a deep sigh or catching at his breath.

"Our worthy president is much excited, at any rate," Reade said to himself.

Finally steps were heard, both by Bascomb and by the pair who watched him. Then another man came upon the scene.

"Evarts, why on earth did you send for me?" demanded Mr. Bascomb, as the discharged foreman came up.

"Because I knew you'd be here——you don't dare do otherwise," was the sneering reply.

"Try not to be impudent about it," advised Mr. Bascomb mildly. "As you may remember, I've had to stand a lot from you."

"And not as much as you might have to stand, either, if I took it into my head to make matters lively for you," jeered Evarts harshly. "Remember, man, you'll do as I want you to do."

"I'm willing to do what I can for you," replied the president. "But——"

"Now, don't throw any of your 'buts' at me," broke in the discharged foreman, roughly. "You failed me in one thing——you didn't make Reade take me back on the job, as I told you to do."

"I couldn't," pleaded Mr. Bascomb. "Prenter stood with Reade and was against me."

"You're the president of the company, aren't you?" Evarts demanded sullenly.

"Yes; but Prenter is a bigger man in the company, and he has more influence with the board of directors. If Prenter came out against me, and persuaded the other directors that I was a bad asset for the company, they'd act on Prenter's suggestion and remove me from the presidency."

"Humph!" jeered Evarts. "Then what would your directors do if they knew that——."

"Stop!" begged Mr. Bascomb hoarsely, "Don't say a word further, man! Sometimes even the leaves on the trees have ears. Don't breathe a word of what you were going to say just now."

Even in the dark the two concealed watchers could see that Bascomb was glancing about him nervously.

"Now, what is up?" gasped Tom inwardly. "What part has Mr. Bascomb been playing in this mystery that he's so afraid of having become public?"

CHAPTER XXI

EVARTS HEARS A NOISE

"I won't shut up," proclaimed Evarts.

"I don't care who hears me."

"But I care," protested the president, in a trembling voice.

"Then you'll have to reward me for whatever silence you want," snarled the wretch.

"Is this blackmail never to cease?" groaned Mr. Bascomb.

"Yes, when you've used me right," declared Evarts harshly.

"Didn't I come forward promptly on your bail?" demanded Mr. Bascomb.

"Sure, for you didn't dare do otherwise. But that only gave me liberty. It didn't put any money in my pocket."

"Are you going to jump your bail, and leave me to pay the bond?" asked Bascomb.

"Perhaps," said Evarts lightly. "You can stand losing the money."

"I suppose so."

"But when I jump," continued Evarts, "I'll have to stay out of the country after that. It'll take money—-and you'll have to furnish me with it."

"How much?"

"Well," continued the foreman, craftily, "I wouldn't leave the country with less than enough to set me up elsewhere. I'd need—-well, let me see. I couldn't start in a new country on less than ten thousand dollars."

"That would make fifteen thousand dollars, in all." Mr. Bascomb finished his remark with a groan.

"Well, what are you howling about?" demanded Evarts unfeelingly. "You've got the money."

"It will lower my holdings in the Melliston Company," complained Mr. Bascomb bitterly "I'm not a rich man, and I haven't any too much stock in the company at the present moment."

"You'd have to sell it all out, if I gave the directors a chance to find out that you're a jailbird—-that you did time as a younger man," sneered Evarts.

"For goodness' sake hold your tongue, man!" gasped Mr. Bascomb in accents of terror.

"Just think," grinned Evarts heartlessly, "how delighted your directors would be to know that you had done time in prison."

"Silence, man!" implored Bascomb. "It wasn't altogether my fault, as you know. And the governor of the state discovered that I wasn't as bad as the jury thought me. It all came through trying to help a worthless friend. Why, man, the governor pardoned me, when I had yet two years to serve and restored me to liberty."

"But you're a jailbird, just the same," jeered the discharged foreman. "Let the directors find *that* out, and how quickly they'd drop you from your office!"

Mr. Bascomb buried his face in his hands and sobbed aloud.

"So," continued Evarts, "I'll give you forty eight hours to raise the ten thousand dollars—-in good cash, mind you—-no checks! Then I'll call on you to hand the money over to me. If you don't, I'll write a note to the directors, telling them to look up your name in the court records at Logville, Minnesota. Now, do you understand?"

"Yes," nodded Mr. Bascomb brokenly.

"And you'll have the money?"

"I—-I'll try."

"You'll have the money—-by day after tomorrow!"

"Yes."

85

"Now clear out—fast!"

"Eh?" inquired Mr. Bascomb, looking wildly at the wretch.

"Get out! Go back to the hotel in Blixton, and don't try to slip away from me at any point in the game. Start—now!"

"Good night!" said President Bascomb in a choking voice.

"Oh, cut out the civilities!" grunted Evarts turning on his heel.

Mr. Bascomb then silently left the spot. His footfalls made so little noise that their sound was soon lost to Dick and Tom.

Evarts appeared in no hurry to leave. On the contrary he drew out a pipe, filled it and lighted it. Then he threw himself down on the ground, puffing slowly.

"From the fact that he sent Mr. Bascomb away, and is himself remaining," thought Tom Reade, "it is rather plain that this scoundrel, Evarts, is awaiting some one else."

The same thought had occurred to Dick Prescott, though, as they lay within thirty feet of where Evarts reclined on the ground, the chums did not deem it wise to exchange even whispers.

After another half-hour Dick pressed Tom's arm. Other footsteps were now near. Then Mr. Sambo Ebony slouched on to the scene.

"Hullo, Tar!" was the ex-foreman's careless greeting.

"Now, doan' get too prescrumptious wid me," warned the black man, with an evil grin that displayed his big, white teeth. "Yo' an' me hab done been good frien's, an' pulled togedder. But Ah want yo' to undahstan', Mr. White Man, dat I doan' allow yo' to call me Tar Baby."

"Oh, come, now, don't get huffy," yawned Evarts, who had not taken the trouble to rise. "I'm not afraid of you, Tar."

"Stop dat!" cried the black angrily. "Yo's takin' big chances, yo' is."

"You're big and powerful, I know that," grinned Evarts. "But I have something with me that makes me just the same size as you are, or perhaps a little bigger. See this!"

The ex-foreman drew from one of his pockets a formidable-looking automatic revolver.

"Huh!" grunted the negro, producing a similar pistol, "yo' ain' no bettah fixed dan Ah be."

"We're quits," laughed Evarts easily, returning his weapon to his pocket. "Put up your rain-maker."

"Den yo' won't call me Tar Baby no mo'?"

"No more."

"All right, den." Ebony put up his weapon.

"Now, what's the programme?" asked Evarts. "You've seen the leader?"

"Yah. Ah's done see de right man. De orders am simple."

"What are they?"

"Misto Reade am to be killed de fust time he show himself," declared Sambo Ebony. "He to be shot down ez soon ez Ah can lay eyes on him. Maybe Ah have to shoot from ambush, but in any case he must be daid befo' de sun go down to-morrow. Our big men am tired to def dat Massa Reade stop do men from havin' a little liquor and playin' cairds evenin's."

"Fine!" thought Tom, with a start. "If Sambo knew how close I am he'd carry out his orders right now! He has his pistol with him."

"An' den, if dey's any fuss made," the black went on, "Misto Hazelton, he done gotta go nex'. Maybe Ah get cotch' w'en I do fo' Misto Reade. Ef dat happen, den dere's anodder man ready to do fo' Misto Hazelton."

"And maybe the second man will get caught, too," suggested Evarts. "Then there'll be two of you with nooses around your necks."

"We maybe get cotch', an' put in de jail," smirked Sambo Ebony, "but doan' yo' beliebe nothin' worse happen. Dere ain' many guards at de jail, an' do gang is on de way. De jail guards done be shot up, an' ouah folks turn' loose. Den we all strike out fo' new place, an' begin all ober again. Den a new gang come in heah and operate to get de money away from de breakwatah gangs. Dere's so much money in dat camp yondah dat ouah folks done gotta hab it ef a dozen men has to be kill'."

"For cold-blooded, systematic villainy I believe I am listening to the limit!" quivered Lieutenant Dick Prescott under his breath.

"They're insane, these people," was Tom's inward comment. "Let this crowd of scoundrels shoot up the jail guards, and do they think the citizens would ever allow the gang to operate in camp? There'd be more likelihood of the known members of the gang being lynched!"

"I won't go back to jail if I can help it," laughed Evarts, speaking to the negro. "As soon as I even up one or two grudges I'm going to slip away."

"Break yo' bail?" asked the negro, showing his teeth.

"That's about the size of it," nodded Evarts.

"Den de w'ite gemman who done fu'nish yo' bond will be feelin' bad, won't he?"

"Let him——he's no friend of mine," grunted the discharged foreman.

"Maybe yo'd like de job ob tendin' to Boss Reade yo'so'f?" hinted Sambo darkly.

"Oh, I'm going to settle with Reade in some fashion," boasted Evarts with a leer. "I don't know that I want to kill him. I'd rather cripple him and let him live a life of misery."

"Thank you!" thought Tom from his hiding place.

"There's another chap we'll have to deal with, too, I'm thinking," Evarts went on. "Reade and Hazelton have a friend of theirs here, and he's likely to make some trouble for us. He's an army officer."

"I done heah'd ob him," nodded Sambo. "We can settle wid him, too."

"We ought to, for he helped arrest me, and he's to be a witness on the torpedo matter."

"W'ate's his name——de ahmy man's?" inquired Sambo.

"Prescott. He's——"

The speaker stopped suddenly, looking about him.

"What was that, Tar?" Evarts demanded.

"W'at yo' talkin' 'bout?"

"I heard a noise, and it was right over there," replied Evarts, pointing to where Tom and Dick lay hidden.

"I didn't heah nuffin'."

"I did, I tell you, and it will have to be looked into," insisted the ex-foreman, drawing his automatic revolver.

"Go ahaid, den," encouraged Sambo, also drawing his weapon. "Ef anybody been a-lis'enin', den shoot him full ob holes!"

Evarts darted at the bushes ahead of his companion. Then an exultant yell came from him.

"Hustle, Tar——and shoot straight! Here are the very people we want——I caught sight of them!"

"Den watch me!" chuckled Sambo Ebony, flourishing his weapon and dashing forward in the tracks of Evarts.

There was no time for the chums to rise and dart away.

CHAPTER XXII

MR. BASCOMB HEARS BAD NEWS

When Evarts used the word "people" he employed it only in a general sense. He had seen no one but Tom Reade, but Tom was the one person in the world whom the ex-foreman wanted most to 'see' at a disadvantage.

"Now, I have you!" Evarts croaked hoarsely, rushing in, flourishing his weapon, then letting the muzzle drop to the position of aim.

Dick Prescott, unseen, stirred almost under the fellow's feet.

Flop! Bump! Caught by the legs, by that famous football player, Dick Prescott, Evarts simply had to go down on his back.

In the same instant Reade leaped, then bent over the prostrate foe.

Evarts was too much dazed to resist much. Tom snatched the revolver out of his hand.

Sambo, beholding this much, came to a dismayed stop for an instant.

"Dick, it's your trade to know how to handle this tool better than I can," Tom cried, passing the captured revolver to Prescott, who swiftly received it as he rose. "I'm afraid," continued the young engineer, "that it's going to be necessary to kill the negro."

"Wow! Woof!" uttered Sambo Ebony. It didn't take that villain an instant to decide on flight. Bending low, the black man ran off with frantic speed.

Dick took a step forward——only one, for Evarts furiously gripped at one of the young army officer's ankles, bringing him down to his knees.

"Hang you, you hound!" ground out Tom, in a rage, as he threw himself athwart of the ex-foreman. Within the next thirty seconds Evarts received a swift, fearful pummeling.

"Let up, Mr. Reade! Let up!" cried the wretch. "I'll behave myself."

"I'll wager you will," retorted the young engineer grimly, as he gripped Evarts by the coat collar and drew him to his feet.

Dick was up and had run ahead some distance. But the time that had been gained for the black man had proved sufficient. Sambo, was now out of sight, nor did he send back any sound to guide his pursuers.

"It may have to be a long hunt for the negro," remarked Tom Reade when Lieutenant Dick stepped back to state the case. "Stand by me and shoot this fellow down in his tracks if he tries to get away."

"Why, what are you going to do to me?" quaked the ex-foreman.

"It's back to jail for yours," Tom informed him crisply.

"Then the laugh will be on you," jeered Evarts. "I'm out on bail—all in regular form."

"You're not on bail on the latest charge against you—attempted murderous assault," Reade rejoined. "Nor will any court allow you out on bail again when Mr. Prescott and I testify to hearing you tell the negro that you were going to jump your bail."

"Humph! That was all a joke," blustered Evarts.

"All right," nodded Tom. "Explain the joke to the judge, if you can find a judge who's a good and willing listener. What you'll find, at this time, is that a hundred thousand dollars' worth of bail won't get you out of jail. Start along with you," Tom wound up, shaking Evarts by the arm that he gripped. "If this sneak tries to get away, Dick, bring him down with a bullet."

"I'm ready enough to do it," Prescott agreed.

A sudden great change came over the ex-foreman. At first he threatened. Then he begged to be turned loose, promising nothing but the best behavior in the future.

"Stop all your nonsense," ordered Reade finally. "There's only one proper place on earth for you, Evarts, and that's behind the bars. Now, move right along, or I'll give you a worse walloping every time you stop or argue."

Finding that nothing would avail with these determined captors the ex-foreman relapsed into sulks. However, he kept walking straight ahead, obeying every order addressed to him.

Tom stopped briefly at the cottage. Mr. Prenter was not there, and Harry Hazelton had turned in. Nicolas was lying on a blanket on the porch.

"You'll have to keep awake until I get back, anyway, Nicolas, and keep your eyes open," Tom informed the Mexican. "Sambo is at large again, and I'm afraid he may turn up here."

"I shall know how to take care of him, Senor," grinned the Mexican holding up his right forefinger.

"That wouldn't help you, this time," Tom retorted dryly. "Mr. Sambo Ebony has a revolver with him. Don't let him get a shot at you; he'd be only too glad to even the score. Now, Dick, I guess we'd better get Evarts over to the jail."

Away started the chums and their prisoner while Nicolas went inside to warn Harry.

Not so very much later Tom and Dick turned Evarts over to the police in Blixton. Evarts was locked up on the new charge. The revolver taken from him was turned over to the police as evidence. The chums also gave their information that they had overheard the ex-foreman tell the negro that he intended to jump bail. But the greatest of all was the news of the plot to rescue the gambler prisoners now in jail.

Then the chums started back to camp.

"I noticed," said Lieutenant Prescott, in a low tone, "that you didn't mention the conversation between Bascomb and Evarts."

"I hadn't any right to," Tom said simply. "If Mr. Bascomb once had trouble in his life, but is living honestly now, it would be criminal of me to expose such a secret that he wouldn't want known. Mr. Bascomb's past is none of my business."

"I'm mighty glad to hear you talk that way about it," said Prescott, resting a hand on Reade's shoulder.

"Why?" demanded Tom rather bluntly. "Did you think that I could feel any other way about it?"

"But Evarts is pretty sure to talk a lot about Bascomb, now," hinted the young army officer.

"If he does," sighed Tom, "I don't know that I can think of any way to stop the fellow."

"Then you don't believe that Mr. Bascomb's evil record of past years affects his honesty now?" Dick went on after a long pause.

"I don't believe it," Tom answered with unusual emphasis. "If I did it would be as much as if I said that a fellow who once makes a wrong step must never hope to get back into the right path again. Mr. Prenter, I am certain, is an honest man and an unusually keen one. He is satisfied to trust Mr. Bascomb as president of the company. But, if Evarts is some sort of family connection of Bascomb's, and if he has often threatened to tell all about Mr. Bascomb's past history, you can imagine the terror that poor Mr. Bascomb has lived in for years."

"If I were in Bascomb's place," Dick declared positively, "I would go before the board of directors and tell them the whole story. Then no one else could ever hold any power over me."

"I guess that's the way all of us think we would act if we'd meet a blackmailer," nodded Reade. "Yet I guess most of the victims, when there's a sad, true story that could be told about them, pay the blackmailer and so secure silence."

"Which may be another way," mused the young army officer, "of saying that most men are cowards. Or, maybe, it's another way, after all, of saying that the man who does anything very wrong or crooked is generally such a coward at heart that he'll spend his savings in keeping his secret from the world."

"Yet Bascomb must have shown considerable bravery in meeting Evarts's demands," suddenly suggested Reade. "Otherwise, Mr. Bascomb would now be a poor man and Evarts would have spent all of Bascomb's money. Heretofore, I imagine, Evarts hasn't been able to blackmail his relative for anything much more substantial than a good job. I hear that Evarts has been drawing good pay from the Melliston Company for something more than four years—-and Evarts isn't a very useful man, at that."

"Then, after four years of easy berths, no wonder Evarts hates you, Tom, for having bounced him out," smiled Dick Prescott.

"I'm afraid I'm going to do worse than bounce the fellow out of a job," sighed Reade. "I'm afraid I've helped head him for prison for a term of a good many long years."

"Evarts did that much for himself," Prescott argued. "I wouldn't waste much worry over the fellow."

"I suppose it's my way to worry over a dog with a sore paw," answered Reade thoughtfully, "Certainly Evarts has done some mean things against me, and without any just cause; but I don't like the thought of his having to be locked up, away from sunlight, joy and life, for so many years as I'm afraid are coming to him."

Arrived at camp, Tom found Mr. Bascomb walking back and forth on the porch of the engineers' house.

"You're up late, sir," was Tom's friendly greeting to the president.

"Yes, Reade; I can't sleep to-night," said Mr. Bascomb wearily. "I came over here to talk with Prenter. Where is he?"

"Asleep, I imagine, sir," Tom answered.

"Wrong," replied President Bascomb. "I've already been inside, but Prenter isn't in the house."

"Then perhaps he thought it too lively around here," laughed Reade, "and went over to Blixton to sleep at the hotel."

Mr. Bascomb didn't reply to this, but puffed hard at the black cigar he was smoking and sending up clouds of smoke.

But the president of the Melliston Company became instantly more distracted when Tom Reade began an account of the capture of Evarts, and his jailing, and the escape of Mr. Sambo Ebony.

Presently Bascomb began to puff harder than ever at his cigar.

"Reade," he finally blurted out, "how long were you hiding there before Evarts found you there?"

"Some little time," Tom admitted vaguely.

More clouds of cigar smoke ascended; then, shaking, and his face a sickly white and green, the president inquired:

"Reade, were you there—-you and Mr. Prescott—-at the time when I talked with Evarts on that very spot to-night?"

There was no use in evading the question, so engineer Reade answered in a straightforward manner:

"Yes, sir. Mr. Prescott and I were there."

"Then—-then—-y-y-you heard all of my talk with Evarts?"

"Yes, sir."

Bascomb's teeth began to chatter so that he was forced to steady his jaws. Tom and Dick looked aside, pitying the man for his evident anguish of mind.

At last the president steadied himself enough to speak.

"Reade, I know I haven't been a very good friend of yours, and I even tried to work you out of this contract altogether. Now, you know my secret, and I'm in your power!"

CHAPTER XXIII

EBONY SAYS "THUMBS UP"

Tom Reade stared in frank amazement at the trembling man.

"Do you mean to insult me, Mr. Bascomb?" demanded the young engineer bluntly.

"Insult you? The fates forbid," replied Bascomb with a sickly grin.

"Reade, I don't dare offend you in any way."

"But you do insult me, sir, in believing that it would be possible for me to make any hostile use of whatever unpleasant knowledge I may possess against you."

"Do you mean to say that you wouldn't use the knowledge?" demanded the president of the Melliston Company.

"You're insulting me again, sir. Perhaps you are to be pardoned, Mr. Bascomb. You have been so long dancing to the fiddling of an Evarts that you don't realize how impossible it is for a gentleman to do a dishonorable thing."

"Then——-then I——-I can rely upon your silence?" demanded Mr. Bascomb, eagerly.

"I am sorry, sir, to think that you even think it necessary to ask me such a question," rejoined Reade gravely.

"Reade! Reade! You can't imagine how grateful you'll find me if I really can rely upon you to forget what you overheard to-night!" cried the humiliated man. "And you, Mr. Prescott——-may I depend upon you, also, to preserve silence?"

"I'm afraid, sir, you're putting me in Reade's class as an insulted man," Dick smiled grimly. "My friend, the people of this country, in the person of their President, have issued to me a commission certifying that I am worthy to wear the shoulder-straps of an army officer. The shoulder-straps stand for the strictest sense of honor in all things. If I depart, ever so little, from the laws of honor, I prove my unfitness to wear shoulder-straps. Have I answered you."

There was silence for a few moments. Then, Mr. Bascomb, having smoked his cigar out, tossed the butt away.

"I'd like to offer you a little advice, Mr. Bascomb, if you won't think I'm too forward."

"What is it?" asked the president, turning briskly upon the young chief engineer.

"Just as long as you both live, Mr. Bascomb, Evarts is likely to bother you, in one way or another. Even if he goes to prison himself he'll find a way to bother you from the other side of the grated door. Mr. Bascomb, why don't you yourself disclose this little affair in your past history to the board of directors? Then it would be past any blackmailer's power to harm you."

"I could tell the directors in only one way," Mr. Bascomb answered, his face growing sallow. "That would be to tell my story and hand in my resignation in the same breath. Reade, you don't realize how much the presidency of the Melliston Company means to me! To resign, or to be kicked out, would end my career in the business world."

In the near darkness a step sounded on the gravel. Then Mr. Prenter came briskly forward.

"Bascomb," said the treasurer of the company, "Reade's advice was good, though wholly unnecessary. There is no need to tell the directors the story of your past misfortune. Most of them know it already."

The president's face grew grayish as he listened in torment.

"Moreover," Mr. Prenter continued, "most of us have known all about the matter since just before you were elected president."

"And yet you allowed me to be elected!" cried Mr. Bascomb hoarsely.

"Yes; because we looked up your life and your conduct since——well, ever since you left the past behind and came out into business life again. Our investigation showed that you had been living for years as an honest man. The rest of us on the board are men——or think we are——and we voted, informally, not to allow one misstep of yours to outweigh years of the most upright living since."

"Knowing it all, you elected me to be president of the company!" gasped Mr. Bascomb, as though he could not believe his ears or his senses.

"Now, let us hear no more about it," urged Mr. Prenter, cordially. "If I listened just now——if I played the part of the eavesdropper, allow me to explain my conduct by saying that I, too, was present to-night when you talked with Evarts. I heard, and I knew that Reade and his friend heard. I listened, just now, in order that I might make sure that Thomas Reade, engineer, is a man of honor at all times. And now, let no one say a word more."

Some one else was coming. All on the porch turned and waited to see who it was. Out of the shadows came a hang-dog looking sort of fellow.

"Is Mr. Bascomb here?" asked the newcomer.

"I am Mr. Bascomb," spoke the president.

"Here's a note for you," said the man, handing over an envelope.

Tom stepped inside, got a lantern and lighted it, placing it upon the porch table. With the aid of this illumination Mr. Bascomb read the brief note directed to him.

"It's from Evarts," said the president, looking up with a quiet laugh. "He commands me to come to him at once, in his cell, and to arrange some way of getting out. My man," turning to the messenger, "are you going back to Evarts?"

"Yes," nodded the messenger, shifting his weight from one foot to another.

"Go back to Evarts, then, and tell him that he'll have to threaten some one else this time. Tell him that I am through with him."

"Huh!" growled the hang-dog messenger. "I believe Evarts said that, if old Bascomb wasn't quick, he'd make trouble for some one."

"Tell Evarts," said Mr. Prenter, "that he can't make trouble for any one but himself, and that he had better save his breath for the next time he needs it."

"Evarts will be awful mad, if I go back to him with any talk like that," insinuated the messenger meaningly.

"See here, fellow," interjected. Tom Reade, stepping forward quickly, "I'm rather tired and out of condition to-night, but if you don't leave here as fast as you can go, I'll kick you every step of the way for the first half-mile back to Blixton! Do you think you understand me?"

"I——I reckon I do," admitted the fellow.

"Then start before you tempt my right foot! I'll give you five seconds to get off."

There could be no mistaking that order. The messenger started off, nor did he glance backward as long as he was in sight.

"You see how easily a chap like Evarts can be disposed of," smiled Mr. Prenter.

"He'll send back again for another try, within an hour," prophesied Mr. Bascomb, wearily.

"If he does," laughed Dick Prescott, shortly, "his second appeal won't come by the same messenger."

"Then you were near us, Mr. Prenter, when Evarts and the negro charged us?" Tom inquired.

"I was," smiled the treasurer. "That convicts me of cowardice, doesn't it, in not having come to your aid at the moment of attack? I wasn't quite as big a coward as I would seem, though. The truth is, I was behind you. Had I jumped in in that exciting moment, you would have thought other enemies were attacking from behind. You would have been confused and would have lost the fight."

"By Jove, sir, but that was quick thinking and shrewdness on your part!" ejaculated Dick Prescott.

"Then you acquit me of cowardice?"

"No," smiled the young army officer, "for I hadn't thought of accusing you of lack of courage."

"I am glad you didn't," sighed the treasurer. "I would rather be suspected of almost anything than of lacking manly courage. Afterwards I didn't make my presence known to you, for, at that time, I didn't want you to know that I had overheard a certain conversation."

"My cowardice has made a dreadful mess of things in a lot of ways, hasn't it?" demanded Mr. Bascomb bitterly.

"That's all past now, so it doesn't matter," spoke up Tom Reade. "We have just one move more to make in this baffling game, and then I fancy we shall have won. When Mr. Sambo Ebony, as I have nicknamed him, is safely jailed I think we shall find ourselves undisturbed in the future. We shall then be permitted to go ahead and finish the million-dollar breakwater as a work and a triumph of peace."

"Every time that one of us opens his mouth," laughed Mr. Prenter, "I am expecting to hear a big bang down by the breakwater to punctuate the speaker's sentence. I wonder whether the scoundrels back of Sambo have any more novel ways for setting off their big firecrackers around our wall?"

"It might not be a bad idea for me to get out on the watch again," Tom suggested, rising. "If I get in more trouble than I can handle I'll just yell 'Mr. Prenter,' for I shall know that he'll be within easy hearing distance."

The treasurer laughed, as he, too, rose.

"My being so near you before, Reade, was just accident. I was prowling about on my own account, when you and your army friend passed me in the deep woods. I had an idea that you were out for some definite purpose, and so I just trailed along at your rear in order to be near any excitement that you might turn up."

"And I suppose you're going to follow us this time, too," smiled Tom Reade.

"Prenter," suggested the president of the company, "what do you say if you and I prowl in some other direction? I've been such a miserable coward all through this affair that now I'd like to go with you. If we run into any trouble I'll try to show you that I'm not all coward."

94

"Come along, Bascomb," agreed the treasurer cordially. "Reade, I give you my word that we won't intentionally follow on your trail."

At a nod from Tom, Dick was at his side. The two high school chums started off with brisk steps.

"Which way are you going?" whispered Dick.

"Let's go down to the breakwater," suggested Tom. "I really ought to visit it once in the night, despite the fact that Corbett is a wholly reliable foreman, and that he has his own pick of workmen on patrol duty there."

As the chums stepped out from under the trees in full view of the breakwater site they beheld the lanterns of the patrol, like so many fireflies, twinkling and bobbing here and there along the narrow-topped retaining wall.

Tom and Dick went out on the wall until they encountered the first workman on patrol. Tom took this man's lantern and signaled the motor boat as it stood in shore.

"All going right, Corbett?" the young engineer hailed, as soon as the "Morton" had come up alongside.

"As far as I can see, Mr. Reade, there's not a sign of the enemy to-night. But of course you know, sir, that we've been just as sure on other nights, only to have a large part of the wall blown clean out of the water."

"All I can say," Tom nodded, "is to go on keeping your eyes and ears open."

"Yes, sir; you may be sure I'll do that," nodded the foreman.

Then Reade and his army chum returned to the shore.

"I guess it will be a wholly blind hunt," Tom laughed, "but I've a notion for returning to the spot where we encountered Sambo Ebony before this night."

After they had left the beach well behind, the chums strolled in under the trees of a rather sparse grove.

Well in toward the center of the grove stood one tree larger than the rest.

From behind this Sambo Ebony swiftly appeared, just at the right instant for surprise. In each hand the negro held a huge automatic revolver.

"Gemmen," chuckled the negro coolly, "Ah jess be nacherally obliged to yo' both if yo'll stick yo' hands ez high up in de air ez yo' can h'ist 'em. It am a long worm dat nebber turns, an' Ah'se done reckon dat Ah'se de tu'ning worm to-night! Thumbs up, gemmen!"

Despite Sambo's bantering tone there could be no doubt that to fail to obey him would be to invite a swift fusillade.

Reluctantly Tom Reade thrust his hands up skyward. Nor did Dick Prescott hesitate to follow so prompt an example.

CHAPTER XXIV

CONCLUSION

"Now Ah reckon Ah'se done got yo'," laughed the big negro, insolently. "It am a question ob w'ich one Ah wantah pick off fust!"

In his wicked joy over having both the young engineer and the army officer wholly at his mercy Sambo, his mouth open and his massive teeth showing white in his grin, advanced nearer.

Yet he did not fail to keep each of his enemies covered. He was watching most alertly for any sign of rebellion on the part of his victims.

Nor was there any doubt in the mind of either young man that the black, after playing with them, meant to dispose of them as his possession of pistols indicated.

He would torment them first, then ruthlessly "shoot them up."

"How long are we to keep our hands up?" asked Tom banteringly.

It would be foolish to say that Reade was not afraid, but he was determined to keep Ebony from discovering the fact.

"Yo's to keep yo' hands up longer dan yo' can keep yo' moufs shut!" scowled the black man, his ugly streak showing once more.

"It makes me think of the way we used to play football," laughed Reade, though there was not much mirth in his chuckle.

"Shut yo' mouf, or Ah done gib yo' plenty to think erbout!" ordered Sambo angrily.

That word "football" set Dick Prescott to tingling. He knew there was some hidden meaning in what Tom had said.

"Are you trying to signal us, Sambo?" queried the army officer.

That word "signal" was intended only for Tom's ear, for Lieutenant Prescott was beginning to guess at the truth.

"On the gridiron, on the gridiron!" hummed Tom, audibly, as he tried clumsily to fit the words to the refrain of a popular song.

Dick Prescott was "getting warm" on the scent of the hidden meaning.

"Shut yo' mouf!" gruffly commanded the lack. "Ah doan' wantah tell yo' dat again, neider."

"Right foot——high foot!" chanted Tom.

Mentally Dick Prescott jumped as though he had been shot. "Right foot—— high foot" had been one of their old kicking signals on the Gridley High School eleven!

Lieutenant Dick Prescott fairly throbbed as he now understood the covered signal.

"Now!" left Reade's lips with explosive energy, though the word was low-spoken.

At "right foot——high foot" and "now" each youth suddenly shot his right foot up into the air.

Tom's landed against Sambo's right wrist, kicking the automatic revolver completely out of the negro's hands.

Dick's kick landed against the black man's left wrist. The pistol held in Sambo's left hand was discharged, though the muzzle had been driven up at such an angle that the bullet passed harmlessly over Prescott's head.

In a twinkling Ebony had been disarmed.

Darting low, Tom grappled with the negro's legs. Then Reade rose swiftly, toppling Sambo over backward.

Dick Prescott bounded upon the prostrate foe, beating him with both fists. Tom also threw himself into the melee.

While the black might have thrashed either youth alone he was not equal to handling both at the same time.

"I've got him, now, and he'll behave, I guess," panted Tom Reade, at last. "Slip off, Dick, and gather in the pistols."

As Prescott did so Sambo made the last few efforts of which he was capable. He had been hammered so hard, however, that Tom did not have extreme difficulty in holding him down.

"Now, lie still and take orders," warned Dick, pressing one of the pistols against the black man's temple, "or I'll get excited and send you out of this world for keeps!"

Sambo Ebony thereupon dropped into sullen muttering, but did not offer to resist. Prescott, as a soldier, had a businesslike way of handling weapons that cowed the black man.

Tom got up leisurely from the prostrate foe.

"Now, you can stand a little farther off, Dick," he suggested, "and then the fellow won't get a chance to tip you over with any trick. If he tries to get up before he's told you can easily bring him to earth again, for you've been taught the exact use of firearms."

"Good idea," nodded Lieutenant Prescott, backing away a few feet. "Are you going to run for assistance now, Tom?"

"No," retorted Reade. "You're going to shoot for it."

"Eh?"

"Fire a shot into the air from each revolver. That, with the accidental discharge of a moment go, will show any listener that there's trouble going on over here. I miss my guess if the shots don't bring help very shortly."

Bang! Bang!

Nor was Reade's guess a wrong one. Not much time passed before steps were heard hurrying in their direction.

"Here! This way!" summoned Tom.

"Are you hurt?" sounded Mr. Prenter's voice.

"No; but we have Sambo Ebony here, and he's going to be hurt if he tries to stir."

President and treasurer of the Melliston Company raced to the spot. Barely sixty seconds afterward Foreman Corbett, with four negroes and one Italian laborer, also came up.

"Corbett, you have the handcuffs I gave you the other night, haven't you?" Tom asked.

"Yes, sir. Here they are."

Tom took the steel bracelets, ordering Mr. Sambo Ebony to turn over and lie face downward, with his hands behind his back. Then the handcuffs were slipped over the black wrists.

"Now, Sambo," called Tom laughingly, "we'll set you on your feet and whistle the rogues' march for you all the way."

"Yah, yah, yah!" jeered one of the negroes who had come up with Foreman Corbett, as he gazed contemptuously up and down the bulky figure of Mr. Ebony. "Yo' done been tellin' us 'spectable cullud fo'ks dat de great way to injye life was to be tough an' smaht, lak yo'se'f. How ye' feel erbout it now? Doan' yo' wish yo' been mo' 'spectable yo'se'f? Doan' ye' done wish dat ye' had been to camp-meeting a few times in yo' life? Doan' yo' wish ye' been honest most er de time, an' been a hahd-wo'kin', pay-ye'-bills niggah lak some ob de rest oh us? Yo' fool lump er tar, yo' boun' ter go de way ob all de wicked——down to ye' grave in misery an' sorrow. It's de way oh all ob yo' lazy, ugly, wuthless kind!"

"I've heard philosophers talk," laughed Dick, in an aside to Tom Reade, "but I can't say that I ever yet listened to a trained philosopher who had the truth of life down any more pat than the negro workman who just now gave his views."

"On all matters of good behavior wise men of all degrees hold about the same views," nodded Reade, "even though they may express their thoughts in differing grades of speech. This good negro knows just where the bad negro has failed in life."

Mr. Sambo Ebony was marched off to jail. Even up to the minute when he was sentenced to twenty years' imprisonment the big black stubbornly refused to give his real name. He was therefore taken away to prison under the name "Sambo Ebony."

Evarts got off with eight years and four months in prison. He is still serving that sentence.

Hawkins and his crew of gamblers and bootleggers were sentenced to two years apiece, as only misdemeanor charges could be preferred against them.

From the foregoing it will be inferred that the proposed jail delivery by other members of the gang from elsewhere did not come off according to plan. The truth was that the citizens of Blixton, when appealed to, organized a strong guard which was thrown around the jail. Doubtless the gang-members were warned in time, and so did not attempt to commit wholesale suicide by running against a citizens' posse.

Mr. Bascomb is still president of the Melliston Company, and he is holding up his head. No further fear of blackmailers oppresses him.

Dick Prescott was able to remain several days longer——long enough, in fact, to see the more substantial structure of the million-dollar breakwater begin to go up just inside the completed retaining wall.

Then Lieutenant Dick was obliged to resume his journey on to Fort Clowdry, Colorado. What happened to Prescott, after joining the army as an officer, is told in "*Uncle Sam's Boys on Field Duty*," the second volume in the "*Boys of the Army Series.*"

Though Harry Hazelton was disappointed in missing some of the excitement at Blixton, he had no occasion to complain in that respect when he and Tom entered upon the next great undertaking of the young engineer pair.

After the disappearance of the big black from the scene there was no further trouble at the breakwater.

Blixton is now an important though artificial harbor. With the completion of the breakwater, and the building of a lighthouse, the next work undertaken was the building of stone docks at which the steamships of the Melliston Line now dock.

The next adventures that befell Tom and Harry were destined to be the most wonderful and exciting of all. These adventures must be reserved for complete telling in the next volume in this series, which is published under the title, "*The*

Young Engineers In The Lead; Or, The stroke That Made Them Masters of Their Field."

It is a story of almost incredible efforts, backed by strong ambition, of two American youths who had both the desire and the will to toil unceasingly and at last reach their goal.

THE END

CPSIA information can be obtained at www.ICGtesting.com
Printed in the USA
LVOW05s1142230214

374826LV00029B/1211/P